RECKLESS IN TEXAS

Metroplex Mysteries Volume II

D1522061

RECKLESS IN TEXAS

Metroplex Mysteries Volume II

Barb Goffman, Editor

Stories chosen by Judges
J Suzanne Frank
Carolyn Kirk
Valerie Wigglesworth

CONTENTS

ACKNOWLEDGEMENT

This is our second anthology, and it's been as exciting bringing these wonderfully talented authors' stories to the world as it was with our first one.

Thank you to Amy Shojai, our chapter vice president, for taking the time to get the manuscript into publishing format and for developing the cover. Thank you to Lori Roberts Herbst, SinC ND secretary and now secretary for Sisters in Crime National, for faithfully lending time to pitch in on cover choice, for updating our website, and for helping with anything where we needed it. Thanks to Jan Angelley, our chapter treasurer, who knows what she's doing with managing our funds and reporting regularly. We also have a wonderful membership. Thanks to all of you for your support.

To the chapter members whose stories were selected: great job! These stories are unique and echo a professionalism in style that make this entire book a work of artistic achievement and enjoyable reading. Our judges, J Suzanne Frank, Carolyn Kirk, and Valerie Wigglesworth, complimented each story as they narrowed them down to the final ten for the anthology. Thanks to all three judges for their time and effort.

Much appreciation also goes to multitalented Terry Shepherd for his impeccable and highly laudable reading of the audiobook version of the anthology. Thanks, Terry.

Thank you, Barb Goffman, for being an editor unparalleled who brings the best out in all the stories and in all she does.

And to John M. Floyd, who is recognized as one of the most published and awarded author of short stories, thank you for liking these stories and writing a foreword about them.

—Barbara Spencer
President, Sisters in Crime North Dallas

FOREWORD

By John M. Floyd

There's just something about Texas.

I don't live there, but I've spent a lot of time in Texas over the years, from Amarillo to Corpus Christi, from Tyler to El Paso, and I not only like the state, I like its writers. I also happen to prefer mystery/crime/suspense stories, so for me this anthology of Texas tales—the second *Metroplex Mysteries* volume—was a double treat.

I think you'll like it too. Most of the stories in this book are whodunits (who doesn't enjoy those?) but every one of them is entertaining and memorable. These ten authors must've known what I like most, because there are surprises and plot twists galore, and characters who are as unique and different as one could imagine (and yes, reckless at times—as the title suggests). The settings and crime scenes are varied as well: elegant mansions, parks, restaurants, interstate highways, bars, nursing homes, insurance offices, RVs, clinics, and cattle barns. The inclusion of some real Dallas and Fort Worth locations and landmarks are icing on the cake, and make the mysteries seem as real as what you'd see on the evening news.

But you don't need me telling you the whys and wherefores of these adventures; you need to see for yourself. May you have as much fun with these ten tales of murder and deception as I did, and may you remember them long afterward. As Carl Sandberg said, "Texas is a blend of valor and swagger." So are these stories.

Read them and enjoy.

—John M. Floyd, January 2023

JOHN M. FLOYD'S short stories have appeared in *Alfred Hitchcock's Mystery Magazine, Ellery Queen's Mystery Magazine, Strand Magazine, The Saturday Evening Post*, four editions of Otto Penzler's best-mysteries-of-the-year anthologies, and many other publications. A former Air Force captain and IBM systems engineer, John is an Edgar Award finalist, a Shamus Award winner, a five-time Derringer Award winner, and the author of nine books. He is also the 2018 recipient of the Short Mystery Fiction Society's lifetime achievement award.

MONSTER

By Shannon Taft

My mother-in-law, Alberta Dolan, did not have an enemy in the world the night she was stabbed to death.

The next morning, a homicide investigator came to notify Robert, my husband of six years. Detective Castillo was kind but professional as she told us what Alberta's twice-weekly maid had found. Still, I was grateful that our au pair hadn't yet returned from taking my son and daughter to visit the Teddy Bear statues in Lakeside Park. At least my children, who were just three and four, wouldn't have to learn about their grandmother's death the wrong way—as if there could be a right one.

When Castillo said she wanted to ask us a few questions, Robert and I agreed, of course. His gait was stilted and his breaths ragged as he led her to the formal sitting room used for guests, but he showed no other emotion.

As for myself, I let my tears run freely. I'd loved Alberta dearly and saw no reason to be stoic about the depth of my loss.

"We understand you have a younger brother?" Castillo asked Robert as she sat on a pink Victorian bustle-back chair.

Robert nodded before easing himself onto the settee opposite her. "His name is Mark. But he wouldn't have done it."

Castillo eyed Robert pityingly. "I understand it's hard to consider—"

"No," Robert said, cutting her off. "I mean that he had no motive. My mother removed him from her will a few weeks ago." Robert huffed out, as if it were an expletive, "Drugs."

Castillo nodded, and I assumed she'd already seen Mark's arrest record. What I didn't understand was why she was asking about Mark at all. Surely she knew that Mark had the perfect alibi? Or did she think his alibi was too perfect—perhaps prearranged?

Robert's lip curled in a sneer. "Mark would shoot up, and Mom would cut him out of her will. Mark would eventually go to rehab, and Mom would put him back in the will. This was the third time she'd written him out, but since he's yet to hit bottom and go back to rehab…" My husband shrugged, as if to say he didn't care one way or the other. "No money for Mark."

Castillo looked around the room. I wasn't sure if she could tell that the sideboard was an original Hepplewhite or that the inlaid table was a William Moore, but since we were in a five-thousand-square-foot house in Highland Park, it was pretty obvious we weren't destitute.

Robert must've noticed her interest, because he said, "My dad passed away ten years ago. Mom was the wealthier one, so she encouraged Dad to divide his thirty-million-dollar estate equally between Mark and me. Mark invested his share in a couple of failed start-ups, then tried to recoup his losses at the poker tables. He's a decent player when he's not high on heroin." Robert's voice got sarcastic. "Of course, you have to be pretty high—or stupid—to gamble away the last of your inheritance. He's been broke for, oh, about three years now."

I tugged on the edge of my long-sleeved shirt. Robert liked to keep the house a cool sixty-eight degrees, which was a little chilly for my tastes. Something in my movement likely caught Castillo's eye, because she turned to me.

"Alberta was a wonderful woman," I said, meaning every word of it. "She was so kind and welcoming when I married Robert." I realized I'd started wiggling my engagement ring back and forth on my finger and held up my left hand to show the investigator the three-carat oval-cut blue diamond. "This was hers, from her own grandmother. Alberta told Robert to use it to propose to me because she wanted me to know we had her blessing."

The detective nodded, but her face was expressionless.

"Was it a burglary?" Robert asked.

The detective assessed him through narrowed eyes. "We don't know yet. Her bedroom looks ransacked, but a lot of valuables were left untouched. And the house's exterior locks don't appear to have been tampered with."

"What about the alarm system?" Robert asked.

"Off," Castillo said flatly. "As for whether the intruder turned it off or it was never on…?" She lifted her hands, palms up. "We're waiting to hear from the monitoring company about that."

"She was always forgetting to activate it," Robert complained. "I told her a hundred times, but she didn't listen. Elizabeth is just as bad," he said, gesturing to me with his head. "I can't tell you how many times I come home late from work and find the alarm hasn't been set."

"Whoever killed Alberta must've been a monster," I said mournfully. "That or horribly desperate."

Robert leaned back against the settee and rubbed the side of his index finger along his bottom lip for a few seconds. "Maybe it was Mark after all. If he was high enough to forget that he'd been removed from the will again…"

Castillo cocked her head. "Your brother was in jail last night, sir. Didn't you know?"

A thundering scowl fell across Robert's face. "How would I know a thing like that?"

My stomach knotted. "Um. He called here. From the jail. He wanted me to ask you to bail him out, but I told him…"

"That I never would," Robert declared. "You shouldn't have accepted the call in the first place."

I knew how angry he'd be about Mark slipping back into his addictions and getting arrested, but maybe my decision to keep quiet about the phone call had been a mistake. I looked down at the rug. From the corner of my eye, I saw that the fringe didn't lay flat, and I wished I could go over for just a second to straighten it.

My head snapped up when Castillo said, "Mr. Dolan, your mother had gray hair."

A crease appeared between Robert's brows. "Of course, she did. She was in her sixties."

Castillo said matter-of-factly, as if discussing the weather, "We found two strands of brown hair in her bedroom, each about four inches long. One was stuck in the dried blood."

Perhaps it was my imagination that she was eyeing my husband's brown hair at that moment, but all the same, I was relieved to have white-blond hair that went down to the middle of my back. Robert always said it was my hair that caught his eyes when we'd first met.

"Mark has brown hair too," I pointed out. "Maybe he got someone else to post bail and he was out last night."

"He never left police custody," Castillo assured us. "He's in the clear."

If my husband had any feelings about that, they didn't show on his face, but his expression became positively wooden when the detective politely inquired whether we were home last night.

"Yes," he said, his voice growing icicles. "Neither of us left the house from when I arrived home for dinner last night—around six—until this very moment."

Detective Castillo scribbled something on her notepad, then asked us a series of questions about people in Alberta's life, including whether there had been any repairmen in her house recently or others who might have noticed a wealthy woman living alone.

Robert and I said that we wouldn't know about repairmen, but that Alberta hadn't told us about anyone showing undue interest in her or the house. "And Alberta would have said something," I assured the detective. "To Robert if she felt it was serious, or to me if she just thought it odd."

"I see," Castillo replied, before moving on to even more questions. I was grateful when Robert answered most of those, but I began to worry that my children would come home before the detective was finished.

I suppressed a sigh of relief when Castillo rose at last, as if preparing to leave.

"Thank you for your time," the detective said. "I expect that I'll have more questions for you later."

Robert stood as well, demanding, "What about the maid? If she has a key, then—"

"Ms. Silva is in a band," Castillo said. "They were performing in a club down in Waco, so she's got a slew of witnesses for the first half of the night, and her bandmates can account for the rest. It couldn't have been her."

"Maybe she gave the key to an accomplice," Robert suggested.

"Perhaps. We can't rule it out yet. But if Ms. Silva was pretending to be shocked, she should win an Academy Award."

● ● ●

Two days later, when the police were finished processing my mother-in-law's house, they asked Robert to accompany them through the place to see what—if anything—was missing.

"Elizabeth should go," he said, gesturing to me. "She'd know better than me what belonged where in my mother's house."

I agreed that was true, and let Detective Castillo drive me to Alberta's house. The entire way there, she kept trying to strike up a conversation about my husband, but I only gave "yes" or "no" answers. If a question required something more specific, I let it go unanswered.

She quickly picked up on my recalcitrance. "Did your husband order you not to speak with me?"

"He didn't have to," I said quite honestly. "Robert has brown hair, and with his brother disinherited, my husband is probably the only person in Alberta's will for any substantial amount. You're a police officer. Every courtroom drama of the last fifty years would tell me not to discuss him with you."

Castillo smiled at me, and I thought I saw respect there.

We arrived at Alberta's house a few minutes later. I emerged from the car and cast my gaze to the stone path along the side of the house, wishing we could go to the back patio, where Alberta and I would often lunch while looking at the peaceful greenery of Turtle Creek and the golf course. Those were my favorite memories of her.

I don't know how long it was before Castillo politely cleared her throat to get my attention. I sighed before following her into the house.

We began with a tour of the ground floor. Everything looked just as it had when I'd taken the children to visit Alberta the week before. When we were done with those rooms, I paused at the bottom of the stairs. I didn't want to go any farther, but Castillo insisted it was necessary.

The detective was right behind me as I trudged up the stairs and made my way down the hall. When I stepped inside the bedroom and saw the blood stain on the thick carpeting, I felt nauseated. Tears welled in my eyes. Alberta had been so very kind to me and was the most fantastic grandmother to my children. We were going to miss her terribly.

Castillo pulled a small pack of tissues from her pocket, handed it to me, then asked, "Do you see anything missing?"

"I... I don't know." I wiped my eyes with a tissue before looking around. My gaze landed on two matching antique dressers, and with a shaking finger, I pointed at the one on the left. "The top drawer of that one should have her jewelry box."

"We found it on the floor." Castillo pulled out her phone and tapped over to a series of photos. "I can show you pictures of the jewelry."

"Can you show me someplace else?" I begged, certain that I could somehow smell the dried blood. "Please!"

"Of course," Castillo said gently.

We went downstairs to the kitchen and she put the phone on the counter. She flipped through the images of the jewelry, giving several seconds to each photo. When she was done, I told her nervously, "It's strange which stuff they took."

"Strange?" Castillo asked, sounding confused. "How so?"

"Alberta had several lovely pieces she'd inherited from her mother and a few from her husband's family. She told me they should go to my daughter, Simone, one day. The heirlooms are... All the heirlooms are in the pictures." I felt my forehead wrinkling as I added, "At least, I think so."

"But some pieces are missing—non-heirlooms?"

I nodded. "She'd bought a set of rubies recently. Earrings and a matching necklace. They weren't so valuable compared to what was left behind, but I know she wore them last month to a gala at the art museum. The theme was fire and ice. And at Christmas, she wore some pearls. They're in our holiday pictures, but I didn't see them in the photos you have here."

"Anything else?" Castillo asked intently.

"I... I think at some point I saw her wearing a set of tanzanite earrings with a matching pendant." I shook my head to convey that I wasn't certain. "Did you contact her insurance company? They ought to have a list."

"We're working on that," Castillo assured me. "But she might not have updated it recently."

I had no idea whether Alberta would've or not. We'd never discussed such things. "Why do you think the killer left behind the heirlooms?" I asked, fiddling with the scarf at my neck.

Castillo said calmly, "For the same reason you're thinking."

"I'm not thinking anything," I lied.

Castillo slid her phone back into her pocket. "Your husband knew he'd get it all in the will. If he stole his family's heirlooms, he couldn't keep them because they'd be proof of his crime. By stealing the newer stuff, he could make it look like a robbery and not lose anything that mattered."

I looked down at the empty counter, not wanting her to see what I feared might show in my eyes.

"Would your mother-in-law have put Mark back in her will if he'd gotten sober?" Castillo asked, turning to lean against the kitchen counter and work her way into my peripheral view.

Robert had already admitted the truth of that, so I lifted my head to face her again. "Yes. I think she would. She did it before. Robert says that Alberta removed Mark each time only to push him into rehab, but I know she was also worried about what would happen to Mark once she was gone. If forcing him into rehab failed, I'm sure she'd have set up a trust so that she could leave Mark some money while somehow preventing him from spending it on drugs."

"Why didn't she do that already?"

"She asked Robert to be the trustee, but he refused. He said he wasn't willing to deal with trying to keep track of when an addict was and wasn't lying about his condition, or to handle Mark's abuse on those occasions when the money would be withheld."

"I see," Castillo said coldly as she straightened.

"We have small children to protect," I explained, certain she'd understand how important that was. "Robert said that Mark would hound the trustee, and he didn't want Mark coming around our house and the children when Mark was high or angry. Robert told his mother to hire a professional to be the trustee, but I think she hadn't found the right person yet. She must've thought there was plenty of time. After all, she was only sixty-three, and a spry sixty-three at that."

I buried my face in my hands, overcome by what my children had lost. Potential years of playing with their grandma. Having her around for all their major life events.

"Was your husband with you between midnight and three a.m. on the night Alberta died?"

My hands slid down my face as I looked up at Castillo. "Robert told you that he never left the house from six—"

"I know what he said," she interjected. "But it's just you and me here now." Her voice grew urgent. "I need you to tell me, was he really home the entire time?"

I didn't feel that I could lie. Not about a thing like this. "I take pills to sleep sometimes. And when I do…" I shook my head. "As far as I know, he didn't leave the house that night. But I can't swear that I would have seen him go."

Castillo patted me on the shoulder and said, "It might not be him. Maybe your brother-in-law hired someone to break in to steal things, and the murder was unintentional. Or perhaps the maid gave the key to an accomplice because she knew she'd have a perfect alibi for the robbery."

I was certain that Castillo didn't believe either of those explanations. Not after what she'd said about Robert when addressing the oddity of which items had been stolen.

"The DNA on those hairs should give us a definitive answer about your husband," Castillo promised. "Until then, if he asks what you and I discussed…" She heaved a sigh. "Tell him whatever he wants to hear. That'll be safest for you."

I nodded, certain that she was right.

● ● ●

The DNA from the crime scene must've taken longer to get tested than it does on television, because it was nearly a month before they got a warrant to force my husband to provide a saliva swab to compare to those results. His lawyer, Joseph Davis, specialized in murder cases and tried to fight the warrant. But since the brown hairs at the crime scene were a 50 percent match to Alberta's DNA, and her only other child, Mark, had already been ruled out as a suspect, it was a lost cause.

Two weeks after the swab of my husband's DNA was collected, he was charged with his mother's murder. The police had tested his sample, as well as one from Mark just to prevent any questions arising at trial. The odds of the crime-scene hairs coming from anyone but my husband were one in nineteen billion. The judge denied bail on the grounds that Robert was a flight risk given his wealth and the weight of the evidence against him.

My husband insisted on having a private lab re-run the tests, which was his right as the defendant. The private lab ran a test using additional loci, which we were told meant locations on the DNA strand. Their test put the odds of his innocence at one in thirty billion. The prosecutor said that he would press for the death penalty if my husband did not accept a plea bargain that carried a sentence of life in prison.

Mr. Davis and I went to visit Robert at the jail and were shown to a private room made available for prisoners to consult with their attorneys. As we waited for the guards to bring Robert to us, Joseph told me, "You have to get him to say yes. He can't win this."

"I… I think he'll listen to you more than me," I admitted as I sat on the bench that was attached to the table. "You're the expert."

Joseph straightened his gray silk tie before taking a seat next to me. I couldn't tell if he was flattered that his opinion counted more than a wife's or worried that the process of convincing

Robert now fell almost entirely to him. He said, "If Robert won't accept a plea, and I have to discuss anything privileged with him, we'll need you to step out."

I nodded my understanding as the door opened.

A guard escorted Robert into the room, gave us all a hard look that implied he wasn't inclined to trust any of us, then went back outside to watch the meeting through a glass window.

Joseph quickly got to the point, which was the need for Robert to accept the plea bargain before the prosecutor could change his mind. He ended by saying, "Life in prison is the best we can do."

"Life?" Robert snarled in outrage. "I didn't kill her!" He pounded a fist on the table, then shot me a glare, as if I was at fault for the lawyer's advice.

I darted a nervous look at the guard, but he didn't seem to think anything he saw was worthy of concern, so I turned to Mr. Davis. "Robert was her *son*," I said, needing the lawyer to understand my husband's position. "I bet his hair, my hair, my children's hair, they're all somewhere in that house. She must've picked it up on her nightgown and…"

"The hair was on *top* of the blood," Joseph said uncompromisingly. "The prosecutor will say that the obvious explanation is that it fell when the killer leaned over her—after she was already down—so that he could stab her a few more times."

"I didn't do it!" Robert screamed, spittle flying from his mouth.

"You had the alarm code," Joseph said, keeping his tone perfectly calm. "You had a set of keys to her house. And you inherit two-hundred-million dollars from her death. That's double what it would've been if you'd waited for your brother to be forced into drug rehab as part of the sentencing for his possession charges. You've already admitted that the rehab would've gotten him back into the will. If you let this go to trial, you will lose. And you will get the death penalty. Texas juries don't like wealthy men who kill their mothers for money. Nobody does."

My husband fired Joseph Davis and told me to find him another attorney. I did, but the new one offered the same advice, so Robert fired him too and told me to try again. Eventually, we found a lawyer, Jim Bates, who wanted the billable hours and media attention of a trial more than he wanted to give reasonable advice.

Oddly, it was hearing Mr. Bates say that Robert should fight the charges that made my husband realize how hopeless his case was. If that camera-hog was the only one to think a trial was a good idea, then it had to be a very bad idea indeed.

"Get Davis back," Robert told me.

I went straight to Mr. Davis's offices and told the receptionist that while I didn't have an appointment, I was willing to wait as long as necessary.

I think she must've heard the desperation in my voice, because she made a few clicks on her computer, then offered to squeeze me in that afternoon.

When I came back a few hours later, it was with a vase of flowers. "Thank you," I told her as I handed it over. "Truly. On behalf of my entire family, especially my children, thank you for helping us."

She looked at me as if I'd lost my mind, and I wondered how many clients spewed abuse at her for being a gatekeeper and never bothered to express appreciation for her assistance.

I was equally effusive when pleading with Mr. Davis to take my husband back as a client. "He sees that you were right. Please, won't you help us with the plea bargain?"

Mr. Davis agreed to represent my husband once more, but it turned out that Robert was a little less convinced than I'd thought. He told Mr. Davis that he would only agree to plead nolo contendere, which meant admitting there was enough evidence to convict him without actually admitting to his guilt.

I apologized to Mr. Davis for the misunderstanding, but he seemed to take it in stride and said, "I'll see what I can do."

Luckily, the prosecutor preferred to claim victory rather than to use up resources on a trial with inevitable appeals, and he accepted the deal. Things moved fast after that, perhaps out of fear that Robert might change his mind. A week later, in accordance with the plea agreement, the judge sentenced Robert to life in prison without the possibility of parole.

An hour after the judge hammered his gavel to mark the end of the ordeal, I filed for divorce.

● ● ●

Robert hired a different lawyer to represent him in the divorce proceedings, but it did him little good. The judge was persuaded by my attorney's argument that I needed the marital assets more than Robert, who would be getting free room and board for the rest of his life. I got twenty million dollars. Robert was left with five.

However, the judge ruled that Robert would not owe child support. Under the "slayer rule," Robert couldn't inherit from Alberta, but she'd left her estate to him *per stirpes*, which meant his descendants inherited instead. My children, Jack and Simone, each got one-hundred-million dollars, and I was made trustee for their funds until they turned eighteen.

Mark threatened to sue Robert in civil court for the death of their mother, but since my children were Alberta's rightful heirs and would therefore have a better claim to any award a jury might grant, no lawyer wanted to take his case. All the same, I felt that something needed to be done.

I sent Jack and Simone to a movie with their au pair and arranged to meet Mark in a very public restaurant at the Village. When I arrived, he was already seated, but he stood at my approach and didn't sit back down until after I had.

He looked clean and sober—and an awful lot like his brother.

I nervously draped a napkin across my lap. "Thank you for coming."

His voice was hoarse as he replied, "Thank you for the invitation."

A waiter came over with menus and asked for our drink orders.

"Just an ice water," I said.

"I'll have the same," Mark told him.

Once we were alone, I didn't even bother to look at my menu. Mark ignored his as well, keeping his eyes on me.

I got right to the point. "I'm prepared to offer you a million dollars—"

Mark shook his head. "No, that's what I came to tell you. I've decided not to sue."

I blinked in surprise. I'd assumed we'd have an argument about my insistence that any money he got would be put in a trust to give him regular payments and that he'd have to show he was sober to get the funds. He hadn't even let me get that far. "You're not here about the money? Then why come at all?"

He paused, and just when he leaned in, as if he was going to answer my question, the server came over with our drinks.

Mark and I sat in awkward silence as the water goblets were placed on the table. The waiter must've picked up on the tension, because he left without asking if we were ready to order.

Mark took a deep gulp from his goblet. When he lowered it, his hand shook so much that the ice cubes rattled. He stared down at the glass, then placed it on the table and looked up at me. "I'm here because of my niece and nephew. I want… I want to be in their lives. To still be their uncle. Jack and Simone are my only family now that Mom is gone and Robert is…" Mark's lips tightened, and just when I thought he was done speaking, he added softly, "Please, Elizabeth."

My children had already lost a father and grandmother, and my parents had passed away before my children were even old enough to remember them. I wasn't eager to deny them an uncle, but I still felt a need to protect them. "You need to stay clean if that's going to happen."

His eyes, so like my husband's, brightened, and his shoulders straightened with seeming resolve. "I will. I swear it!"

He certainly sounded convincing, but I heard in the back of my mind Robert's warnings to his own mother about trusting an addict. Perhaps there was a way to accomplish more than one thing with this meeting. "If you agree to waive all claims resulting from Alberta's death, I'll put five-million dollars into a trust for you—"

"This isn't about money!" Mark insisted.

"Maybe not," I allowed. "But Alberta would want you to be okay financially, and after everything she did for me, Jack, and Simone, it's important to me that I honor that." My plan had been to start negotiations at one million and work up from there, but his request had changed the tenor of the meeting. "You won't have access to the principal, only the interest. I've found a trustee who'll deal with everything, including the drug testing that you'll have to pass each month to get your interest payments. We'll use those same tests to determine if you'll be permitted to see the children. As long as having you in their lives is healthy for them, I won't restrict your access."

"Thank you," Mark said fervently. "For all of it." He leaned against the back of his chair and gave a long exhale. "Do you remember, at your wedding, when I gave a toast and said you were too good for my brother?"

I'd been so nervous that day, I remembered little of it. I gave Mark a smile that I hoped conveyed some form of fond reminiscence.

Mark said firmly, "Truer words were never spoken, Elizabeth. I had no idea then just how right I was."

After the last of the legal and financial matters were finalized, I went to visit Robert in prison. I felt he should know firsthand what I'd done and why.

As it turned out, he already knew the most important thing. The one thing I couldn't send anyone else to tell him.

When I lifted the phone on the opposite side of the plexiglass barrier from him, the first words out of his mouth were, "You killed my mother."

I suspected that the prison recorded all visitor communications, and I'd wondered how to tell Robert the truth without incriminating myself in any way. I tried not to show my relief that Robert had made my carefully practiced hints unnecessary. "What are you talking about?"

"You had access to my hairbrush. You had access to my key ring. You knew the alarm code, not that Mom remembered to turn the damn thing on. But you would've been prepared if you'd needed it."

I kept my face blank and hoped any cameras watching me would record my reaction as one of shock. "Is this some sort of game to get a new trial? Because I won't lie for you, Robert."

"You had those sleeping pills you'd use when the pain kept you up at night. You must've put one in my dinner that night."

I'd had those pills on hand to cover the pain from his beatings. And I'd put several, not one, in his meal. I'd have put it in his nightly whiskey, but I'd feared it might noticeably alter the taste. "I have no idea what you're talking about."

"I told you I'd kill you if you ever tried to leave me."

He had. He'd also threatened to kill our children before he'd let me take them away. That was the night I'd decided to get out from under him. To make sure he could never follow us.

"Why did you kill my mother? Why not murder me instead?"

Because I was not an idiot. All those long-sleeved shirts to cover the bruises from when he'd grab me by the arm and twist. The collection of scarves to hide more bruises on my neck and shoulders. The spouse is always a murder suspect, and once the police looked closely at me, it wouldn't have been hard to figure out my motive. But I'd had no apparent reason to murder his mother, who'd never been anything but kind to me.

At some point after Robert's sentencing, he must've finally calmed down enough to examine the situation. I looked at him and saw that he understood that his lifetime of imprisonment had been my way to ensure I could safely divorce him. He was simply hoping to get me to admit it on tape.

"I loved Alberta," I said with complete honesty. "As for your attempt to blame me for her death…" I gave a shrug and watched the anger flare in his eyes on the other side of the plexiglass barrier.

But his anger could no longer hurt me. The authorities weren't going to be interested in his theories when they already had someone in prison for the crime and no evidence against me. And while my offer to Mark had been driven as much by my guilt as my desire to obtain an ally, it ensured he'd be uninterested in helping a brother who'd wanted him cut off. Overturning Robert's conviction—and thereby the legal procedures that had followed—would only serve to endanger the financial trust that I'd established for Mark.

Reminding myself that the conversation was likely being recorded, I chose my words with care as I stood, preparing to leave Robert for the last time. After everything I had said and done since Alberta's death, I had some experience telling the truth while misleading listeners. "Robert, do you remember when Detective Castillo came to tell us that Alberta was murdered?"

"What of it?" Robert demanded.

"I told her that whoever killed Alberta must've been either a monster or horribly desperate. I still believe that, Robert. I always will."

An attorney from Washington, DC, **SHANNON TAFT** enjoys writing mysteries with a twist. Her most recent short stories include "The Perfect House" in the *Restless Spirits* anthology, "Research" in *Hook, Line, and Sinker*, and "It's Not Tennis" in *Black Cat Weekly* #52. When she's not writing, Shannon enjoys hiking (operating on the theory that chocolate has no calories as long as you're wearing trail boots) and photography (because she can take one thousand snaps and pretend the single one that looks good was the result of her immense talent).

THE PRIME WITNESS TO THE MURDER OF DR. MALACHI SAMSON

By Derek Wheeless

5:25 p.m.

Y ou are the one," the detective said. His voice carried none of the usual bravado that championed the powers of his intellect. Rather, this time, his words were soft and mournful. "You are the one who killed Dr. Malachi Samson."

He closed his eyes, drew in a long breath, and took three steps away from me. After several lengthy beats of silence, his eyes opened, and he reviewed me, adjusting as he did the thick spectacles on his nose. Still, I thought, they looked crooked, and I decided I was tired of looking at his glasses.

He pointed to me, and I stole a furtive glance at the confused stares from the other three women in the room, the heat rising in my face. "You weren't afraid he would die," he said. "You were afraid one of them would. And one-quarter of his millions was better than none of his millions. And yet, what I find most curious about this episode is this: you needed none of his money. Your own wealth is vast. A mere glance at this beautiful old Georgian mansion will attest to this fact."

The detective was ill-informed. True, I had inherited a substantial amount decades ago when my father passed, including this beautiful old house. But I also had inherited his taste for the refined, particularly when it came to the world of literature, and collecting the finest, rarest books in the world had cost me millions. The house and its contents notwithstanding, I was the least well-off of anyone in the room, including the little detective.

He paused to compose himself. "You had the motive, and you provided the means when you offered him and all of us your sourdough cookies. And by having this gathering at your house, you provided yourself with the opportunity. I believe it was Miss Wilkie I heard only a few hours ago noting how fortunate she was her beloved Dr. Samson hadn't expired in her own domicile. No, it happened here, at Havenwood, because this is where you had control."

I looked around the room. Havenwood. It was more than just another beautiful old mansion on Dallas's Swiss Avenue. She was a friend I could trust and with whom I'd always felt safe. I had taken care of Havenwood, meticulously, and in return, she'd cared for me through every loss, setback, and unfulfilled desire. A woman without a husband needs a place to rest her broken heart on occasion, and I'd rested mine in Havenwood for nearly thirty years. I had needed Havenwood, and she had needed me. And we both had needed the good doctor's money.

The detective leaned in closer, lowering his voice. "And you alone knew I would be here, for you were the one who called me. Your plan was laid with excellence aside from one minor detail, which, as it turns out, was your undoing, and that was in calling me. I was to be your alibi. Instead, I am the prime witness to the murder of Dr. Malachi Samson. And you are under arrest for his murder."

I felt my shoulders sag as I looked around one last time. Such a beautiful big old library, born from deep mahogany and polished brass. The expansive, rare first-edition mysteries on the shelves had taken a lifetime of collecting, their worn pages giving the room those wonderful musty notes of cut grass and fading vanilla. I'd spent priceless hours in here by my grand Elizabethan marble fireplace poring over my collection. I was going to miss my library. And I was going to miss Havenwood.

He had me. I knew it because I knew the policeman's record was spotless. He was a stickler for detail. In that, we were the same. He always got his man. Always. And this time he would get his woman.

"Well played, Detective Crumbächer. Your powers of deduction and reasoning remind me of your old man." I extended parallel wrists to him. "I am at your disposal."

Twenty minutes earlier

"One of you in this room is a killer."

A deep pall fell like a heavy black veil over the face of a grieving widow.

"And I am sorry to say I know the one."

I narrowed my eyes at him, as if I might divine his very thoughts. Was he bluffing? Was it too late to make my escape? Where in the devil's name would I even go? I could never leave my beloved Havenwood, and I decided to hear what this little round man said, and then I would determine my fate if the power to do so still lay with me.

The detective continued. "I was invited here, not as a guest of honor, as one might presume, nor as a friend, for the one who summoned me was manipulating me. No, I was a pawn, not here only to witness some happenchance death, but, more importantly, to give credence to the alibi of the very one who had caused that death. My purpose lay solely for the sake of the murderer."

I turned to the others. They were glaring at me, hating me. But why should they? I had just made them wealthy women. I'd done the dirty work for them, and they were recompensing me with the most ungrateful of spirits.

Detective Crumbächer continued, and we refixed our gaze on him, our mouths slightly agape with concern, real and otherwise. He pointed to each of us in turn. "One of you is a killer."

Such prolonged melodrama. He hadn't named me, but we all knew whom he was talking about. His performance annoyed me as much as his confounded cockeyed glasses.

Miss Goznel, her rather large body sprawled across an oversized brown leather sleeper, threw back her head, fanning herself with fat fingers. "I don't like any of this. I want to go home."

"No!" The detective's booming voice reverberated across the shelves of the palatial library. No doubt it was the emotion of the moment. I understood. I've often done the same. He took a deep breath, smiled, and nodded an apology for his outburst and began again, softer this time. "No one will leave. We will see this through to the end. The killer must have her comeuppance, the deceased his justice."

He strode across the room, lifted a glass decanter, helping himself to a glass of whiskey. I'd never known him to be a drinking man, but this was a ghastly situation for him, one I suspected he'd never encounter again, and I sympathized with his plight, fighting the sudden urge to request a glass be poured for me as well.

I studied Miss Cantwell and Miss Wilkie, who sat huddled together on an early twentieth-century settee I'd just had reupholstered in dark-green velvet the previous week. I thought the new addition looked exquisite in the library. The women, on the other hand, with their fingers clasped in frightened solidarity, for what reason I knew not, looked absolutely dreadful. Their eyes were swollen and red. Their matching platinum-dyed power bobs were a frazzled mess. And each wore the most ordinary matching navy-blue dress and soutache jacket, quite suitable for the plainest of wakes, but in my opinion only added to their dismal, tired look.

As for me, I determined to be neither fearful nor sullen regarding the situation at hand. I would not be like some forlorn young schoolgirl who'd been caught writing something nasty on the bathroom wall and was now awaiting her day of judgment in the headmaster's office. There is a certain decorum that must be followed among the educated and privileged, particularly a woman with my standing, and I had always refused to break ranks with such responsibility and tradition.

"I'm going to do something no man should ever be obliged to consider in a woman." The detective stroked his long black beard thoughtfully as he spoke, his eyes closed. "I'm going to surmise the four of you are all approximately the same age. Late forties, perhaps? Early fifties?"

The little round man had surmised correctly. We nodded our affirmation without a word.

"I presumed. And respectfully may I add you all continue to look quite remarkable. I, on the other hand, two decades your junior, am often confused with being much older, even middle-aged." He rolled his hazel eyes and sighed. "A little extra weight and a beard can do that for a man. Nonetheless, I readily admit to being an old soul much like this beautiful house. A vintage taste that for some may be difficult to acquire."

He took another sip of the brandy, then deposited the glass on the table behind the couch, where I sat, my legs and arms crossed.

"Dr. Malachi Samson was in his seventies, was he not?"

He didn't wait for us to answer. He knew that we knew that he knew.

"About three decades your senior. And it was he who formed this, how do you call it, Malachi's Women of the Arcane? You were his *girls*. Stop me if I'm wrong." He smiled and waited, and when none of us detoured him, he pulled from the right pocket of his jacket one of the sourdoughs I'd served my guests only hours earlier. I hadn't seen him take one, and I wondered when it'd become his.

"A plate full of cookies, each of them laced with the killer drug, but fatal to only one person in the room." He took a bite of the cookie and wiped his lips with the red pocket square he'd lifted from the breast of his coat. He smiled satisfactorily. "My favorite cookie. There is nothing better than a simple sourdough. I grew up with them. It seems I've eaten them all my life." He slipped the remainder of the cookie into his mouth and shrugged. "See? It doesn't hurt me. You all enjoyed one or more as well. I know. I watched you. It didn't hurt you. And it might even make you more, shall we say, receptive to certain pleasures, just as it's intended for some men. But it killed Dr. Samson, because inside each of these cookies is a killer dose of ground Viagra. I am certain of it."

From his left pocket he lifted a small clear evidence bag. Inside was one of my sourdoughs. "It will be tested. But I don't need testing to be certain that Dr. Samson would've known better than to mix sildenafil citrate, the main ingredient in any erectile-dysfunction drug, with his nitroglycerin, which contains nitrate. It's a deadly combination, which is why it concerned me when I saw the prescription bottle but no pills within. I knew he wouldn't have taken it, so where would all those little blue pills go?" He patted his side pocket again.

The little round man stroked his beard and raised one eyebrow. "But the bottle had to be there, by the bed, as if he and his murderess had made love only hours earlier, because she knew the toxicology report would find the sildenafil citrate in his system, and there had to be a reason. And it would make sense. He was, after all, in his late seventies. How else, it would be presumed, would he be able to keep up with, not to mention satisfy, the needs of a much younger, very fit, beautiful woman?"

Miss Goznel jumped up from her seat, an accomplishment that required some time and considerable effort on her part, considering. "It was her, wasn't it?" She pointed a fat finger to me, then sank back onto the leather chair, obviously worn out from her sudden demonstration.

The detective looked at Miss Goznel, then in turn to each of us. His eyes lingered on mine longer than they had on the others, uncomfortably so, I might add. And I, begrudgingly so, nodded. He lifted his eyes heavenward, and we watched as he began to pace the room, hands clasped behind his back. "*Alea jacta est*, Miss Goznel." There was a deep sadness in his words.

He stopped in front of the flickering fireplace, adjusting a log with the poker. But I knew his mind was elsewhere.

"First, I gave you the motive for the murder of Dr. Malachi Samson. And now you have the means of this extraordinary killing, the cookie laced with sildenafil citrate. But you want more from me? Ah, everyone always wants more from Detective Virgil Crumbächer. Perhaps, I think, you ask too much of me now. Very well, I will give you your killer, the only one who had the opportunity to cause his death."

He crossed the room to where I had taken my seat on a walnut-colored leather couch with rolled arms and deep tufted buttons. Behind me was a large polished wooden table stretching the length of the couch. He reached behind me and lifted his glass from the table, drained its contents, returning the glass to its original location. I saw the look in his face. This wasn't an enjoyable job for him, but, nonetheless, a necessary one, and one, I had to admit, in which he excelled. He extended an arm to help me stand. I smiled and placed both of my hands in his, and we faced each other, our bodies only feet apart.

Then he frowned at me, and I knew what he was finally going to say. And I knew he was sad.

Ten minutes earlier

"He wants us to meet him in the library." Miss Wilkie's words were cold and without emotion. "He said he would reveal the killer." She raised an eyebrow, just one, before turning on her heels.

It was then I realized I had never really liked Miss Wilkie.

I paused to consider the moment and took one more bite.

The little detective. Always the showman, always seeking to be the center of attention in his personal life. I'd heard, through my various social circles and board positions, of his penchant for the professional spotlight too. It was said he was as much thespian as he was detective. Considering that he'd now called us all to the library to accuse someone—not me, I hoped—in front of witnesses, I most certainly agreed.

I pushed myself away from the table. The rest of the chicken-salad sandwich would have to wait. I stood and wound my way through the house to the library.

● ● ●

Thirty-five minutes earlier

For what seemed like a full half hour I could not find the detective. It was as if he'd vanished, disappeared into some hidden labyrinth beneath this grand old monstrosity of a house. I went room to room searching for him, only to find Miss Goznel, Miss Cantwell, and Miss Wilkie sitting in the front parlor, their chairs pulled up in private conversation. When I approached, their whispers stole away and they offered only eyes of condemnation. My suspicion was confirmed when Miss Cantwell flat out asked me if I was to blame.

"You can't be serious?" My shock was real, not because I hadn't done the deed, but because I had erroneously assumed my compatriots would take it for granted our dearly departed leader merely had died of a heart attack.

"From what I hear, he arrived before the three of us," Miss Wilkie said. "You could've poisoned him, put something in his tea, rat poison, or…" She turned toward Miss Cantwell. "What's that drug people are always dying from in Agatha Christie's novels?"

"Cyanide, dear," Miss Cantwell said.

"Cyanide?" My shock was even greater now. "Have you lost your marbles? One can't just go to the druggist and buy cyanide these days! A hundred years ago I grant you. But to your point, no I did not put cyanide in his tea."

"Then why was Dr. Samson already here before the rest of us?" It was Miss Goznel this time, and her chubby little cheeks were flaming red, and that bothered me. "The doctor has never been on time for our meetings, and yet today when I arrived—and as you all well know, I am always the first in the group to arrive, as I pride myself on being extremely punctual—the doctor and the detective were already in the library chatting." She fanned her reddening neck with her hand. "When, pray tell, did he arrive this morning?"

I drew in my breath, raised my eyes upward, and pursed my lips, as though carefully weighing the words about to leave my mouth. In truth, I'd practiced both the prose of my next line and the pose accompanying it before the bathroom mirror each night this past week prior to bathing.

"The doctor arrived some time before the detective. I had some first editions I wanted him to peruse before I showed them to you all."

"Was that the *only* reason you invited him to arrive before the rest of us?" Miss Wilkie asked. "Miss Goznel's question is warranted. The doctor's early arrival is quite a departure from his normal cadence." She lowered her face and stared at me over her wire-framed readers. "I think you owe us the full truth."

"Let's just say…" I smiled and let out a sigh of deep satisfaction. "The good doctor had certain needs for which he often turned to me for assistance. It's all quite natural, of course."

There was an audible gasp from the other three, but I knew to a woman their astonishment came not from the revelation that the doctor and I had been intimate that morning. Rather, their histrionic embarrassment was quite expected of them as genteel southern women.

"How's it possible?" Miss Wilkie asked, her arms now crossed. "He hasn't been able to get it… I mean to say, he hasn't been able to perform in over a decade."

She looked at the other two, and they obliged her generously by the fervent nodding of their heads.

I provided them the most perfect Cheshire cat smile. "I have my ways."

When I whirled to exit, to my utter amazement the famed detective was standing in the doorway of the parlor, and his glasses lay at the most deplorable cockeyed angle across his face. How long he'd been there and how much he'd heard God only knew. Nevertheless, I weighed the possibilities and determined the unexpected moment lay in my favor. If he'd heard enough, I had just provided even more credibility to my alibi. Perhaps his clever eavesdropping would persuade him to dispense with any suspicions he might have otherwise developed.

A sheepish grin spread across my face. Curiously he did not return the smile. Rather, he slipped away into another part of the house, and I chose this time not to look for him. Instead, I made my way to the kitchen.

Opening one of the glass refrigerator doors, I scanned the prepared sandwiches my cook had assembled the day before. I suddenly found myself ravenous, and a chicken-salad sandwich seemed just the thing.

I'd taken the smallest of bites when Miss Wilkie came bursting through the kitchen door.

● ● ●

One hour earlier

Our little cadre had only just adjourned when Detective Crumbächer asked if he might have a private word or two with me.

"It's merely a matter of procedure," he said, the fingers of both hands laced in front of his chest. "There is the tiniest of details I must ask you about. It is, however, quite delicate in its nature, particularly for a man in my position and a woman in yours."

I assuaged his fears and reminded him we were both adults.

"It has to do with the master bedroom," he hinted. With his arm extended he invited me toward my room. There, with as much flair as I perceived necessary, I gave the room a bit of a frantic look as though I may have forgotten to store away some rogue piece of naughty lingerie.

"I do hope you will forgive the mess," I said, feigning concern over the slightest bit of untidiness. Truth be told, there wasn't one item in the room out of place. I had made sure of it. I believe the movie directors call it product placement.

The detective pointed toward an opened prescription bottle sitting on the nightstand next to a small tube of intimate lube. I scurried to the nightstand and scooped up the lube, slipping it into the stand's drawer.

I gave my guest a silly grin. "I'm embarrassed, to say the least."

He waved it off. "Not at all. Very natural, of course. My concern is with the prescription."

"Yes?" This was another moment I had spent hours rehearsing before my bath.

"The label says the bottle contains Viagra, and yet I find none of the little blue pills inside."

I shrugged. "I suppose Dr. Samson took his last one this morning."

He grimaced. "I don't understand."

I gave him a questioning look.

He went on, "When the medical examiner reviewed the body of Dr. Samson, he discovered nitroglycerin in his pocket, and the doctor would've known the fatal consequences of mixing these two scripts. Most curious."

"Quite!" I admitted with grave concern.

I stole my chance to turn away from the uncomfortableness of this awkward exchange. I now saw how problematic this was for the detective—and for myself. Why would Malachi take the Viagra if he was also taking nitroglycerin? I felt my heart sink. The fact was, he wouldn't, and I found myself, for the first time that day, at a slight loss for words. And yet, I needed to say something, anything that might give the detective the slightest bit of doubt regarding the doctor's wisdom that morning.

"Perhaps he didn't…" I began as I spun back.

But when I looked for Detective Crumbächer, he was gone. He had simply vanished from the room without a sound.

• • •

Twenty-five minutes earlier

"You can't be serious!" I knitted my eyebrows together and searched the detective's face, not for answers, for those I had, but for the questions I assumed he had.

He went on. "Who is Dr. Samson's beneficiary?"

There was a long pause amongst us.

Miss Cantwell was the first to recover. "We all are."

"The four of you?"

"Yes," she said. "We were, well, as he put it, *his girls*. We are Malachi's Women of the Arcane in more ways than one."

She let that sink in for a moment, and I watched as the detective caressed his black beard with long downward strokes. He turned his eyes toward me and cocked his head. The detective had questions.

I drew in a breath. "Let me explain. We all met decades ago at a bookshop Malachi owned at the time in downtown Dallas."

Much of this the detective already knew, but I understood his appreciation for thoroughness. "We were all a lot younger then, Malachi only in his fifties. He took a fancy to us, one by one, and each of us shared with him a love of reading mysteries and discussing them. The four of us began meeting with him in our homes to have book talks and guest speakers. And we called ourselves Malachi's Women of the Arcane. The MWA." I released a little chuckle, more, I knew, from the nervous tension I felt than from the humor of my recollection. "We even began calling ourselves by our last names, just as though we'd stepped right out of a Golden Age classic."

I paused for just a moment for this next part was going to be slightly awkward, even for me. "We also shared other interests with him as well. Suffice it to say we enjoyed each other immensely."

It was Miss Goznel who spoke up now. "At first, none of us knew about the others."

The detective's face turned to each of our faces, and in turn we nodded our agreement.

"Are you saying Dr. Samson was having a tryst with each of you at the same time yet unbeknownst to the others?" he asked.

"We found out about each other quite by accident," said Miss Wilkie. "He sent one of us a text meant for the other and, well, we began to talk."

"We were furious when we found out," said Miss Cantwell. "We had become great friends. Meeting in each other's homes to discuss our favorite mysteries. Until then, we each thought we were the only one he was carrying on with in secret."

"At the very next meeting," said Miss Goznel, "we confronted him. And what he said surprised us."

The detective waited for Miss Goznel to continue, and when she didn't, I determined it was my turn to pick up the story's thread. "He gave each of us a copy of his will. Each of us was to receive exactly one-quarter of his estate. Malachi was a very wealthy man even then, worth millions more now. What were we to do? Turn down millions because he liked to spread his seed more than most men?"

"Margie, please!" Miss Wilkie scolded me. "Detective Crumbächer, you have to understand, we were all widows. Each of us lost our husbands early in our marriages. None of us had a lot of money, well, except for Margie. We felt taken care of by Malachi, and he, being an unmarried bachelor, seemed to enjoy his new role as provider. But of course, he had certain needs, and well, so did we. So, rather than disband, as we were initially inclined to do, we continued on as Malachi's Women of the Arcane. And we have been so for the last two plus decades."

"So, you all benefit from his death?" the detective asked.

"On one condition," said Miss Cantwell. "If one of us four women died before he died, the entire will was to become null and void."

Detective Crumbächer looked to me again.

"Malachi loved us, no doubt. And I believe he genuinely felt we all adored him. I don't think he ever feared for his own life. He knew that we knew the money would one day be ours," I said. "But he was also an avid reader of murder mysteries, and he didn't want one of us murdering the others for a bigger share of the estate. If we plotted no ill will toward each other, we each would inherit millions and millions from him."

"He just had to die first," said Miss Cantwell.

A grave look came over the detective. "And now we have motive."

* * *

Ten minutes earlier

The detective found me in the sunroom poring over a mystery about a group of seniors in a retirement village who'd gotten mixed up in a murder investigation. I found it a delightful read.

"May I have a word with you and the other women in the living room?" he asked.

"Of course," I said and set my book down, immediately regretting I hadn't slipped a bookmark inside. I also regretted I'd answered him so quickly and without the least regard for the specifics of genuine mourning. I was, after all, one of four grieving women, as it were, and our beloved had actually died in my very own home. I'd have to be more careful around the detective.

I followed him into the house, and when we were all together, he said, "I am terribly sorry for your loss today, ladies. I know this has been a great shock to you. Death has a way of stealing into our lives at the most benign of moments. It's most unfair."

The tears began to flow amongst the women, and I remembered to cry too, this time.

Miss Wilkie was the first to improve. "I am grateful Malachi didn't die at my house." A sudden look of alarm came over her. "This meeting *was* supposed to be at my house!" Her tears began to stream again. "This is my month to host the meetings." She turned to look at me. "If you hadn't asked if we could have the meeting here…"

I furrowed my brow. "You're right!" I turned to the little round detective. "I had some new first editions I just had to share with our group and asked if I could host this week instead of Miss Wilkie."

Miss Wilkie was inconsolable now, her face planted in both hands. "I…don't know…how I would even be able to… I would have to move… I couldn't live…anymore." She looked up at me. "You poor…thing! Will you move?"

I placed a tender hand on the side of her face. "No, my dear. My mettle is not quite so thin as all that. For your sake, I am glad it was here at Havenwood where he expired. And doing what he loved best, discussing mysteries. So, no, I won't leave."

"I must insist none of you leave this house anytime soon."

The detective's voice was surprisingly firm, and we all gave him our rapt attention.

"For the time being this house is an active crime scene," he said. "I have just been speaking with the medical examiner, and he is not convinced the founding leader of Malachi's Women of the Arcane died of natural causes. There are, you might say, some peculiarities about his death. It is quite possible your beloved Dr. Malachi Samson was murdered."

● ● ●

Two hours earlier

It took a while for the medical examiner to get to Havenwood. Once he arrived, I reminded him and his team to be mindful of the hardwoods and the orientals and the books. This had been, by design, a very clean murder, and I intended to keep the mess and the chaos to a minimum.

I didn't see much of the detective for a couple hours after the doctor died. I supposed he was doing what all policemen do when someone dies. Filling out reports, asking questions, or, in this instance, answering questions as a firsthand witness to the doctor's death, which is precisely why I'd invited him in the first place.

As for me, I busied myself with shedding tears and sharing remembrances of the doctor with the three other women. When that became tiresome, I slipped away to find some place to be alone. My beloved library was off limits as it was the scene of the incident. So, I rallied myself and headed to the sunroom. The sun's rays felt good on my skin as they poured through the glass panes in the ceiling, and I picked up a book lying nearby, *The Thursday Murder Club*, and began again where I'd left off the day before.

● ● ●

Forty-five minutes earlier

It was right in the middle of Detective Crumbächer's suggesting that most murders are crimes of passion when Dr. Malachi Samson dropped the plate of sourdough cookies and fell from his chair, his body making a deadening thud as it smacked the oriental rug lying neatly over the polished hardwood.

We all screamed while the detective jumped into action, kneeling over the victim, checking his pulse, attempting CPR, and finally announcing the leader of our book club was dead.

I knew Malachi would have approved of his murder.

Twenty minutes earlier

"Our main attraction requires very little introduction," I said, "which is all well and good because I happen to know how very much he detests any and all pomp and circumstance."

The five of us offered our gracious applause until Detective Crumbächer raised a hand in humble acknowledgment. Then he began, speaking of his life as a detective for the Dallas Police Department, his meteoric rise through the rank and file of Dallas's finest, and of the intellectual methods he uses in catching the basest of criminals.

I found the talk mostly routine. The subject matter wasn't altogether unfamiliar to me. I'd heard him speak on prior occasions. The most interesting part was his confounded glasses. They just wouldn't stay on his face in a level position.

I looked at my watch. The death of Dr. Malachi Samson was at hand.

Thirty minutes earlier

The last of my guests finally arrived, and I assembled them all in the library.

"You have such a wonderful old library, Margie," Miss Wilkie said.

I beamed. It truly was the centerpiece of Havenwood, which is why I'd chosen the library for our final meeting. It seemed fitting Malachi's murder would take place in the most fabulous mystery library in Texas, maybe anywhere, though I had heard of a gentleman in New York whose library might've rivaled my own at one time. That notwithstanding, I knew Malachi would've been pleased to know, had I'd made him privy to my plot, that within the hour he would be killed while surrounded by the most magnificent first-edition tomes in the world, each regaled for its murder, its suspense, its plotting of clues and red herrings. Was there a finer genre in the world of literature? I didn't think so.

"You are most kind, Miss Wilkie." I picked up a plate of cookies I'd set on the table behind a walnut-colored leather couch and offered it to the others. "Care for a small snack as we prepare to be thrilled by our famed Detective Crumbächer?"

Each of the women took one. The detective politely declined. I imagined he did not want to discuss the nits and nuances of crime fighting with a mouth full of sourdough, and I applauded his decision.

I was pleased to see the good doctor took two of the cookies, and I immediately offered him two more. He smiled and nodded, and I slipped him a wink I knew the others would see.

Miss Goznel raised her hand, as though we were in school. "Dr. Samson, I never saw you arrive. Did Margie sequester you away somewhere in this beautiful old mansion earlier this morning?"

I answered before the doctor could clear his mouth of cookie. "The good doctor and I had…some personal topics to discuss before everyone's arrival." I gave the group a coy look, well-practiced. "Now, if everyone is ready, perhaps we should get started with today's talk."

10:30 a.m.

The doorbell rang its familiar Westminster chime, and I scurried to answer it. It would be my second guest to arrive, and my favorite, not to mention my most important. I had delicate work to do today, and the one on the other side of the door would see me through. He had to. It was his duty, now, and in my estimation, always had been.

I swung open the door, and there he stood, all five feet five of him. Bless his heart. Round and plump, the only qualifiable inheritance from his father. A full black beard disguised his face. I found it quite distasteful, but what can I say these days? And those grotesque black spectacles on his nose. Always at a slight angle, as if one of his ears were higher than the other. I knew for a fact that wasn't the case.

I clasped my arms around him. "Darling! Just the man I've been waiting for!"

He smiled and gave each cheek a kiss. "Hello, Mother. You look as stunning as ever." He entered Havenwood's grand entryway. "I've had this appointment on my calendar for over a month now, and yet you've been so coy about even the smallest of details. Please, do tell me what this is all about. What is the big surprise?"

"Thank you, darling. I try. You are sweet to notice. This is the reason you're my favorite son. And to answer your question, *you* are the big surprise! I have designs on you today. The three other women of Malachi's Women of the Arcane will be here soon. Our illustrious leader has already arrived. And you are to be the guest speaker of our little soiree. I know I've kept you in the dark, and I know how busy you are with your work, but do as I say, be a good boy, and grace us with one of your fine talks on fighting crime."

My dearest son raised both arms feigning arrest. "No need for the hostilities, Mother." He extended his wrists to me in mock resignation. "I am at your disposal."

DEREK WHEELESS lives in Frisco, Texas, and graduated from Baylor University. Derek has been a public classroom teacher and school administrator. His short story "Think of the Children" appeared in *Malice in Dallas*, the Sisters in Crime North Dallas chapter's first anthology. He has also had a Young Adult noir novel published, *We Planned a Murder*. Derek is a member of Mystery Writers of America, Sisters in Crime, Sisters in Crime North Dallas, Private Eye Writers of America, Society of Children's Book Writers and Illustrators, The Author's Guild, and Alliance of Independent authors. Learn more at www.DerekDWheeless.com

TRACTION

By Terry Shepherd

It was the kid or me," Homicide Detective Jessica Ramirez told the nurse. "The decision was simple then. But I'm having second thoughts."

And third thoughts. Six days ago, Jessica had been chasing a suspect, who'd thought he could beat an oncoming car. Jess had shoved him out of the way, leaving her to take the full brunt of the impact. And that is why she was lying in room 404 at a Dallas hospital, chatting with her nurse while glancing at Pequeño. Yep, she'd actually named the tiny spider weaving another parabola in the slowly splaying web at the far corner of the off-white ceiling, not that she'd admit it to anyone.

Get me out of here, Pequeño. Before I lose my mind.

"Just three more weeks in traction, Jessica. You'll be back chasing bad guys before you know it."

Rachel McCabe's sunny disposition did nothing to diminish Jess's frustration. The nurse smiled at the spider before pressing a needle into Jess's suspended leg. No matter how good the shooter, Jess thought, cortisone still stung. She didn't like how narcotics dimmed her mind, refusing every pain killer except Motrin, so she felt every sensation.

"You're a veritable goddess, Rachel. You have the means to chase any dream, yet you're still swapping bedpans and listening to whiney babies like me."

As Rachel's face clouded, Jess regretted making assumptions about the daughter of Dallas's richest man. Jess had gotten to know Rachel somewhat well during the time Rachel had been one of her primary nurses, but she clearly didn't know everything.

"I wish," Rachel said. "My father says I need to design my own destiny, just like he did. 'Challenges create character,' he tells me. 'And money means more if you've earned your own.'"

The cloud lifted. "And I will."

The nurse popped the syringe into the red sharps box by the door. "Almost have enough saved to go back to college in microbiology. Life among the test tubes is where it's at."

Jess studied the remnants of her bland hospital lunch. It sat next to her bed atop an adjustable table, along with get-well cards and a foam cup filled, as usual, with more crushed ice than water.

"I'll give you a hundred dollars for a bag of nacho tortilla chips."

Rachel put her hands on her hips. "Loaded with potassium. Bad for you."

The swing of the door distracted them both. "How is Dallas's toughest lady cop?"

The voice belonged to a lithe older woman who could have easily graced the cover of the magazines Jess avoided at the grocery store. Perfectly styled blond hair spilled over the shoulders of a designer dress. Bright-red fingernails matched her lipstick. Jess thought there was a little too much foundation on the woman's face. But Jess preferred to wear hardly any makeup and realized how little she knew or cared about those details.

"Mother-daughter lunch, Mrs. McCabe?" she asked. The McCabe women ate lunch together several times a week.

"We're off to one of Rachel's favorite twigs-and-sticks bistros," Melissa McCabe said. Her words were punctuated by the charm of affected laughter that fit her role as one of Dallas's top socialites.

Rachel rolled her eyes. "Healthy food helps you enjoy a longer life, Mom."

Her mother ignored the subtle dig, forcing a beauty-pageant smile in Jessica's direction. "I hear they caught that horrible kid you were chasing. If I were you, I would have focused a little more on my own safety and less on some jail-worthy delinquent."

Jess got a better look at the smile. There was a hint of a wince when Melissa McCabe displayed it.

"Some days, ma'am, I would agree with you. And, Rachel, you're blessed to have zero competition for your mother's affection. My sister's adventures seem to consume much of my mom's time."

Melissa waved the notion away. "Ahh, but it is I who have the competition now. Rachel has been keeping company with Nathan Carroll." She exhaled in resignation. "Her father and I just wish the boy had more prospects."

Jess's cop sense wanted more details.

Rachel's eyes narrowed, releasing invisible darts at her mother. But the nurse's voice still bubbled.

"You're all set, Jessica. We're off for some twigs and sticks. I'm taking vacation this afternoon to deepen the mother/daughter bond." From Rachel's tone, Jess wasn't optimistic. "Keep healing."

With that, the two women vanished, leaving Jess to deal with her thoughts.

A detective's mind never shuts down. Jess was constantly scanning for puzzles to solve. They appeared in the edge of a remark or the nuance of a glance. Years of experience had taught her to see the tip of an iceberg in the blink of an eye.

Something was odd about the McCabes.

The family patriarch was a legend in Dallas business circles. A ruthless personality who demanded a return on every investment. Even the beneficiaries of his philanthropy had confided that Ethan McCabe could be a bully.

The flinch in Melissa McCabe's smile revealed a person trying to hide pain. As Jess played back the memory, she noted a slight darkness beneath the foundation by the woman's right eye.

If I peeled away that war paint, I bet I'd find a bruise.

Rachel was bruised too, Jess suspected, but on the inside, thanks to her parents' focus on her boyfriend's financial prospects. Nathan Carroll came from another notable Dallas family, but prominent for different reasons. When Nathan was a child, their once prosperous business fell on hard times. The father, a brilliant software engineer, committed suicide, leaving his wife and adopted son to fend for themselves. Jess could imagine Ethan McCabe's reaction when he learned his daughter was keeping company not just with the son of a vanquished competitor but one with an uncertain heritage. From everything she'd heard about him, Ethan McCabe was the type to care about bloodlines.

Jess felt the twitch of a bedsore and tried to adjust her body amid the ropes and hooks that elevated her shattered right leg. She fought the subsequent shooting pain by returning her focus to the spider. Another circle woven. Inexorable progress creating a trap that would provide both exercise and nourishment.

Well, Pequeño, at least one of us is doing something productive.

Rachel didn't show up the next morning. But Jessica's partner, Detective Alexandra Clark, did. And she had news.

"Old Man McCabe died last night," Ali said, leaning against the corner wall beneath Pequeño's ever-expanding web. "The medical examiner says heart attack, but that's preliminary."

Ali flicked her eyebrows, always a precursor to some delicious detail. "And a rookie found a pillow with a facial indentation."

Jess could imagine how excited that rookie must be about discovering such a juicy bit of evidence. "Are you thinking murder one?"

"Who knows? Everybody hated the guy. Our list of suspects could encompass most of the Dallas County population."

With her mind engaged, Jess's pain softened.

"I assume everything goes to the wife?" she asked.

"Yup. They had a prenup back before they were cool. At least the woman did one thing right."

"If someone did off the guy, who would be on your list?"

"The wife, of course. Word is they fought like cats. And Ethan McCabe was a former Golden Gloves champ. I wouldn't want to be near those fists if he lost his temper."

The hint of a bruise beneath Melissa McCabe's eye came back to Jess.

"Then there's the daughter, Rachel. She must also stand to inherit. Money and motive go together like butter and popcorn," Ali said.

Jess tried and failed to scratch an itch beyond her reach. "The mom is hiding bruises beneath her makeup. Battered women kill more men than angry kids."

Ali's phone vibrated. She took the call while Jess contemplated Pequeño's web and imagined the McCabe women and Nathan Carroll spread-eagle in its middle.

"Some news," Ali said when she hung up. "Turns out there's a witness and a video. They've invited Nathan Carroll for questioning."

* * *

"Save a felon's life and bust your leg. That's a news story."

Lyle Cunningham, of *The Dallas Folio*, grinned the next morning as he opened the newspaper to page three, depositing a zippered plastic bag of hard candy on the table next to Jessica's bed. The editor, publisher, photographer, and chief reporter of the city's weekly free throwaway bowed. "I come bearing gifts.

But only for a few minutes. Congressman Boyle got drunk and drove his pickup into the Texas Book Depository a few hours ago. Gotta get some pictures."

There's always someone with a camera, Jess thought. She accepted the newspaper, which had a good-size article about her "accident" last week. The adjacent photo took up a quarter of the page. It caught the instant where she was airborne, with the car skidding to a stop and the perp's legs spinning in blurred circles like a cartoon character on the run. She'd heard a witness had videotaped her chasing the suspect, but until now she hadn't had the pleasure of seeing the end result. She shuddered and closed the paper.

Cunningham stole a piece of candy from the bag, popping it into his mouth. "If Ethan McCabe hadn't bought the farm the night before last, you would have been page one this week."

He held his phone up and aimed it at Jess like a camera, having stepped far enough back that he surely had her cast and the hospital bed in the frame. "I need some good day-two stuff for next week's issue. Say Cheese!"

"I do NOT give you permission to shoot or print photographs," she barked, sending her right leg into stratospheric pain.

The editor clicked anyway, and Jess twisted her head down, trying to ruin the shot. Her eyes fell on the newspaper. McCabe's face peered at her from the front page, beside photos of his wife, daughter, and her boyfriend. "What's the real backstory on the McCabes and the Carrolls?" she asked, looking back up, just as the editor took another picture.

"Do I have permission to use the photo?" He swung his phone around so Jess could see the result. It was not a flattering likeness.

"Talk to me and we'll see." She hoped he knew something she didn't. Considering all his sources, he very well might.

"Once upon a time, the men were tight. Partners. They had a falling around the time the Carrolls adopted the kid. McCabe eventually struck gold with a computer software patent, and Bruce Carroll shot himself. Oddly, the wives are still friends. But on the sly. The old man wouldn't tolerate any contact. The kids' love affair must have made him crazy."

"And the Carrolls' son?"

"Smart as a whip and a hard worker. He's got a temper, though. I hear he almost came to blows with Ethan McCabe when the guy nixed the kids' wedding plans."

Jess studied the head shots of McCabe and Nathan Carroll. There was something about them she hadn't noticed before.

"Too bad the Carrolls couldn't have kids."

"Word is the wife wanted kids, and the husband didn't. Andrea Carroll even left her man for six months. But he must have come around. She came home, and before you knew it, they'd adopted. Told friends it was a compromise. Too bad their happily ever after was short-lived. A mere two years later, Bruce Carroll was dead."

"You love sordid stories, don't you, Lyle?"

"What true ink-stained wretch doesn't? It's too bad McCabe didn't bless the kids' union. He might still be alive."

"You think Nathan killed him?"

"I hear the video is a little hard to see—dark—but clear enough for a DA to ask questions."

The editor cocked his head. Jess knew the move. He was waiting to deliver the zinger.

"But…?"

"But there are twenty patrons at a who swear Nathan Carroll was with them all evening. The bar has security camera footage from five angles to back 'em up."

"So, Nathan walks."

Cunningham nodded. "Likely. Besides, I hear your ME says heart attack. The autopsy won't be released for a few days, but

Jannalynn Willett is about a sharp as they come. If something was amiss, she'd find it. McCabe had other health issues. He was an insulin-dependent diabetic. Even though his daughter was a nurse, he hired a practitioner to give him his daily shot. Ethan McCabe didn't trust anyone he wasn't paying."

More questions were forming in Jess's mind. Queries Lyle Cunningham couldn't answer. She took a last look at the photos on page one, folded the paper, and put it next to her on the bed.

"You earned my permission to use that ugly photo you took," Jess said. "But next time I do something stupid, can we agree to keep it out of the public record?"

Jess saw Cunningham steal a glance at his watch. Her time was up.

"Never," he said. "You're my favorite subject."

Jess waved the reporter away. "You say that to all the girls. Do me a favor. See what you can dig up on Nathan Carroll's adoption."

Cunningham rubbed his chin. "Hmm. Very interesting. You're working on a theory."

"Data, my dear Watson. It is a capital mistake to theorize without it."

"I'm on the case, Ms. Ramirez. See you in the funny papers."

As Cunningham sashayed toward the door, Jess picked up her cell phone and sent a text: "Jannalynn. Call me when you have a second. Got a medical question."

* * *

It surprised Jess to see Rachel McCabe back on duty. The nurse appeared shortly after Cunningham's departure, holding a tray with a pair of Popsicles on it.

"Who's up for a snack?"

Rachel acted as if it was just another day at the office. Her bright eyes and disarming smile were as sprightly as ever.

Jess couldn't hide her puzzlement. "What are you doing here?"

"No sense in spending time with the dead when you can help heal the living." The nurse set the tray on the wheeled table beside Jess's bed, then unwrapped the Popsicles.

"Rachel. You just lost your father. It's okay to take time for yourself."

"OK. I'll grieve for ten seconds." She handed Jess a grape Popsicle, then held up her own twin one. "A toast. To my father's metabolism, for seeing fit to release us from his abusive grip."

Rachel bit off a large chunk of her frozen treat, just as her pager sounded, a high-pitched beep like an insistent sparrow. Rachel read the screen and sighed. "Someone needs an enema." She took two large bites, finishing off her Popsicle, and deposited the bare stick on the wheeled table. "Back in a few minutes."

When Rachel cleared the doorway, Jess set her ice pop on the tray, dumped the candy out of its Ziploc bag, and slid Rachel's Popsicle stick into it, sealing the package and slipping it behind her pillow.

Her phone vibrated. She recognized the caller ID.

"Dr. Willett, I presume. Any chance you can swing by and visit me? I need a favor."

Dr. Jannalynn Willett's fame as a soap maker equaled her growing reputation as Dallas's often-unconventional medical examiner. She placed a sample of her artistry on Jessica's nightstand. A child could easily mistake it for a scoop of vanilla ice cream in a sugar cone.

"I love it when the little stinkers who steal my stuff take a lick," she said, flopping into the recliner at the foot of the bed. "Even smells like the real deal too."

"You are twisted, Jannalynn. Are all MEs like this?"

"We dance with dead people, Detective. It warps the brain. How much longer until they cut the strings on that leg?"

"Three weeks. If I don't go crazy first."

The ME put a finger against her temple. "Let me guess. You're bored and want to know what I think about the McCabe autopsy."

Jess laughed as she glanced at her door, confirming it was closed. "Twisted and smart."

"Takes one to know one."

"So, are you really calling it a heart attack?"

Jannalynn leaned back. Her gaze seemed to settle on Pequeño for a moment. "We weave our webs with the knowledge we have, Jess. All his body parts were in the right places. The guy's insulin level was low for someone who just got his daily shot, but what's normal is a pretty broad range in that department."

"Any chance he was smothered?"

"Ahh. The pillow. There was no stress on the trachea. No petechial hemorrhaging in his eyes. His lungs were clear."

"Nothing else out of the ordinary?"

"McCabe had hyperkalemia. That's what probably killed him, the underlying cause anyway. I talked with his primary, and the doc says that was one of his many likely tickets to the hereafter. Diabetics sometimes do that to you."

Jess didn't recognize the word. "What's hyperkalemia?"

"High potassium. You gotta keep that stuff under control or you're a candidate for…"

The ME waited for Jess to finish her sentence.

"Heart attack."

"Bingo, Doctor Ramirez. Case closed."

Jess was beginning to believe that the McCabe case was far from closed.

"Want to help me with a little side hustle, Jannalynn?"

The ME's eyes lit up. "The plot thickens?"

"Just testing an idea."

Jess produced the Ziploc bag.

"A tongue depressor?"

"A Popsicle stick. I bet it has saliva on it. I've been fooling around with AncestryDNA, and it got me thinking… Let's analyze it. Off the clock and unofficially for now, if you please. Think you could get a DNA sample from Nathan Carroll? Look for a match?"

Jannalynn rubbed her hands together. A sly smile spread across her face. "Ancestry? Sounds like fun. And I think I still have our boy's coffee cup from my good friends at homicide. They are pack rats. So, whose Popsicle stick is it?"

"Let's wait and see what the results say."

The ME put the bag in her purse. "It'll take a while, but you'll get what you need."

"You're my favorite accomplice, Jannalynn."

Jannalynn tilted her head as she smiled. Jess could see the wheels turning.

"What do you know about McCabe's insulin?" the ME asked.

Jess thumbed through Ali's messages. She was stuck in traction, but her partner was keeping her apprised of the case. "The drugstore delivered it to the house that week as usual. McCabe required it be kept locked up. Only the nurse practitioner and her backup had the key. One of them came over every morning and night and administered it."

"Locked up?"

"The guy was neurotic."

"Maybe with good reason."

Jess nodded.

"What about the night McCabe died?" Jannalynn asked.

"The daughter says that the nurse did her thing as usual. She was there. Saw it. Ali says there's no reason to suspect the nurse."

"And the wife?"

"Out to dinner with Andrea Carroll. Turns out that those two were each other's alibis. The staff at the restaurant confirms it."

Jannalynn stroked her chin. "Nice and tidy."

Jess closed her eyes. Puzzle pieces danced in the darkness. When she lifted her lids, she pointed to the spider web, glad she'd rejected an orderly's offer to remove it.

"A perfect circle of evidence," she said. "The only really odd thing about all this is the neighbor across the street and her grainy video. She saw a woman leave the house—the nurse, I think—and then Rachel left about ten minutes later, at which point a man went inside. The neighbor had noticed him standing down the street, watching the McCabe house, so she grabbed her video camera. Ali says the tape's dark, but it looked enough like Nathan Carroll to raise questions. Too bad there are a bunch of semi-drunk patrons and a very sober set of security videos that show Nathan enjoying himself at a bar at the same time."

Jannalynn shrugged. "It's a conundrum."

Jess had to agree.

"Was Nathan a regular there?" the ME asked.

"Nope. The head bartender said it was the kid's first visit. Apparently, Nathan prefers sports bars. I guess we all try something new from time to time."

Jess squinted at the rays of the afternoon sun. The window glass cast a rainbow prism across her elevated leg as the puzzle pieces fell into place.

Jannalynn gave Jess one of her patented piercing stares. "You have this figured out, haven't you?"

The pain in Jess's leg returned. "Let me know when you get that DNA analysis. And thanks for the soap artistry. It will hold a place of distinction when they spring me from this traction prison."

The final puzzle piece was in Jannalynn's hands. Until Jess had it, there was nothing to do but watch Pequeño string more circles in his own web. And wait.

Three weeks had passed, and the manila folder that Jessica had compiled about the McCabe case was almost complete. Lyle Cunningham had come through with some interesting information about Nathan Carroll's adoption. He'd agreed to keep it quiet when Jess promised to call him first with tips for the next twelve months. More stories were emerging, detailing Ethan McCabe's abusive behavior. *The Folio* painted him as "The Most Despised Man in the City."

Cunningham had also run an article saying that Melissa McCabe and Andrea Carroll would now share joint ownership of McCabe Software. That was funny, Jess thought, considering Melissa still opposed linking the two families by marriage. Her daughter's ability to maintain a sunny disposition had become strained.

Meanwhile, Ali had reported that some of the DNA on McCabe's pillowcase matched Nathan Carroll's. But the DA had decided against an arrest. Twenty witnesses against a nosy neighbor and dirty linen.

At 10 a.m., the doctors cut Jessica's leg free of the traction torture chamber, wheeling her to the plaster of paris room, where an ankle-to-thigh cast was encrusted over her leg. One more night of observation and Jessica would gain her freedom.

A text from Jannalynn Willett was waiting for Jess when she returned from the cement factory: "Sent the info to AncestryDNA under your name and mine. Guess what? We're related…and I'm a man!"

Jess opened the ancestry app on her cell phone. There was a message there too. An unfamiliar name with a familiar face who wanted to connect with his newly discovered relative.

Jess called Andrea Carroll. She needed confirmation. The conversation lasted over an hour.

Satisfied, Jess told Ali everything, asking her to bring both the McCabes and the Carrolls, including Nathan, to her hospital room at seven p.m.

Jess studied Pequeño's artistry. The spider's trap was nearly two feet wide. It entangled a half-dozen unfortunate insects, all dead. Pequeño looked bigger and stronger because of the sustenance. Jess was feeling her own strength return.

The stage was set. Now it was time to weave her own web.

● ● ●

Room 404 felt even more claustrophobic when filled with Jessica's guests. Andrea Carroll got there first and took the recliner. Rachel and Nathan entered, holding hands, followed almost immediately by Melissa McCabe. The three sat on less comfortable wooden chairs Ali liberated from other rooms. Jess's partner closed the door, leaning against it in case any of the players felt the urge to bolt.

Jess lay on her bed, propped in a sitting position. It felt good to have both legs resting on the mattress.

"Thank you all for coming," she said, making eye contact with everyone. "I think you know why you're here."

There were feigned expressions of confusion (with fear mixed in) from everyone except Andrea Carroll. Jess expected this. Liars are the worst actors, she thought.

"As you all know, the medical examiner and Dallas County district attorney have determined that Ethan McCabe died of a heart attack. 'Natural causes' is how *The Folio* reported it. The community has accepted this as fact."

Jess focused on Melissa McCabe and Andrea Carroll. "But facts can sometimes be misguided perceptions, perceived as truth.

"If you'll indulge me, I'll tell you a story about a cold-blooded homicide. If we agree that it's true, it will not leave this room." Jess tapped her case folder. "If there is any dispute, Detective Clark will make an arrest on the spot and all of this information will be shared with my superiors and the press."

Rachel began chewing a fingernail. Nathan crinkled his brow. Their mothers remained stoic.

"Twenty-seven years ago, two men worked together on an idea. A tiny package of ones and zeros that could revolutionize software development. One was the visionary. Another knew how to turn the idea into a fortune.

"But techies have a natural distrust for bean counters. And our idea man kept the secret to himself, revealing only enough to give his partner something to sell."

Jess's gaze turned to Andrea Carroll. "A husband's long nights in front of a computer screen must have been a lonely experience, Ms. Carroll. Who could blame you for being susceptible to another's affection? The only problem was that this other man happened to be your husband's partner."

Nathan and Rachel snapped their attention in Andrea's direction, eyes wide, mouths agape.

"Nerds often marry other nerds," Jess continued. "You were smart enough to understand what all those ones and zeros meant. Perhaps in the heat of passion, you let enough slip so your illicit lover understood their meaning. In return, he gave you a gift. A seed that mixed with your contribution to create a life."

Jess turned to Melissa. "Betrayal's sting encompasses all involved, Mrs. McCabe. I don't know what heated conversations took place, but I believe that both marriages were never the same thereafter. You couldn't forgive your husband for what he did—and not just to you. He froze out his partner. Mix destitution with depression, and suicide can become an appealing escape. Surely your husband knew that. Ethan McCabe committed murder in the worst possible way. Totally untraceable. And the only two women who might bear witness had powerful motivation to remain silent."

Nathan's soft voice cut in. "What happened to the baby, Mother?"

Jess held up a hand. "Allow me. Your mother and I had a long conversation this afternoon. Bruce Carroll was sterile. His whole family knew. So he and your mother decided that the best way to avoid scandal was for Andrea to pretend to separate from Bruce, then give birth in another state. She and Bruce would then 'reconcile' and adopt you from the agency she left you with. They got a nice payment for their services."

Jess turned to the nurse. "One year after that, you were born, Rachel. Nathan grew to adulthood. And as boys often do, he fell in love. But his adoptive parents never told him the truth about his biological backstory."

Jess held up the issue of *The Folio* with Ethan's and Nathan's headshots side by side on page one. The resemblance was now unmistakable. She could see the full meaning of her narrative dawn on Rachel. The nurse slowly pulled away from Nathan, the reality of their connection sinking in.

Nathan put a hand on his mother's shoulder. His voice was that of a small boy. "Mom… Why didn't you tell me?"

Jess continued. "Somehow, Andrea Carroll and Melissa McCabe made peace with one another. My enemy's enemy becomes my friend? Naturally, a marriage match between their two children was problematic. Ethan McCabe couldn't have blessed the idea if he wanted to."

Jess pointed to Melissa. "But your hatred for your husband grew with each passing year. His physical abuse naturally added fuel to the fire, but the flames of infidelity ignited it. You wanted him to die for his sins."

Melissa McCabe gripped the arms of her chair until her fingers were a ghostly white.

Nathan jumped to his feet. "She didn't kill him. I did. I smothered the monster in his sleep. I'll admit it to the authorities right now."

Melissa's hands relaxed. She took a deep breath and spoke up. "That can't be true. Twenty people saw you elsewhere at the time of Ethan's death."

Jess exhaled. "Ahh, yes. How can someone be in two places at once? Thanks to a Popsicle stick and a cooperative medical examiner, I had a pair of DNA samples sent for testing, using our own names as aliases. The analysis confirmed your sibling relationship." She gazed at Nathan and Rachel. "But it also revealed something else."

Jess turned her cell phone screen so everyone could see an open email on it. "Nathan, does the name Nicholas Carpenter mean anything to you?"

Nathan collapsed into his mother's arms. Head in hands, he wept.

Andrea Carroll rubbed her son's neck. "I'm so, so sorry Nathan. There were two babies. Identical twins. We planned to take both home, but there was a mix-up at the agency, and when we arrived, you were the only one left. I wanted to tell you this afternoon so you wouldn't have to find out like this, but I couldn't find the words."

"I'm glad I killed him," Nathan wailed.

Jess's voice softened. "You did smother him, Nathan. But you didn't kill him. Your sister did."

Rachel's face morphed into a sneer. "You can't prove that."

Jess flipped through the folder to a report from Ali. "'Rachel McCabe testifies she witnessed the nurse practitioner give her father his insulin shot.'" Jess turned her attention back to Rachel. "You'd avoided your father since his rejection of your suitor. Why were you there that evening?"

"I wanted to convince him to change his mind about Nathan. I…" Rachel looked at the man she now knew to be her brother. "I loved him."

"Potassium chloride, Rachel. Remember our conversation about potassium. It can be deadly. And it was, when you distracted your father's nurse practitioner and switched vials."

Melissa made a weak attempt to go on the offensive. "A good lawyer will tear this speculation to pieces, Detective Ramirez."

"Perhaps, Mrs. McCabe. But only if it goes to trial."

Jess had everyone's attention. Time elongated to a standstill until she uttered four words.

"Tell me the truth."

Andrea spoke. "What Jessica says is true. I told her as much on the phone today."

"Why would you do that?" Melissa asked.

With a shrug, Andrea said, "I trust her."

Rachel deflated. The arrogance vanished. "I distracted Dad's nurse and switched the vials. I watched him die after the nurse left. Nathan must have come into the house afterward." She looked to her brother. "You can't be convicted for killing someone who was already dead."

Nathan wiped wetness from his face. "And I found Nick the same way you did, Detective Ramirez. I never told Mom because the agency wouldn't give us any information about our birth parents, and I didn't want her to think..." The tears flowed again. "That I didn't love her."

His voice strengthened. "But we both hated Ethan McCabe for what he did to my father. I may not remember Bruce Carroll, but I grew up believing he was my father. McCabe denied me him." Nathan caressed Rachel's hand. "And he wanted to deny me Rachel too. Nick learned my mannerisms and played me to perfection that night at the bar."

Jess looked at her partner. Unspoken communication so common among police detectives flowed between them. Ali finally nodded.

Jess studied each face. It was time for judgment. She became a cop to see justice done, to soften suffering. Perhaps this unconventional solution could do both.

"There is no benefit in deepening wounds." She shot the nurse a penetrating stare. "But murder is serious business, Rachel. If the district attorney somehow finds evidence to pursue charges, it will force me to share mine."

Rachel nodded. "But what about the man my father killed? Who pays for Bruce Carroll's death?"

"Considering your father is dead, I'd say he paid. Later than he should have, but he paid."

Jessica looked up at the empty carcasses hanging on Pequeño's web. He did what he did to survive. Perhaps he wasn't much different from the group before her.

"We can't change the past," she said, closing the file. "May you all create a better future…together."

TERRY SHEPHERD is the author the Jessica Ramirez Thrillers, The 221B Club stories for mid-grade readers, and the Readers Views award-winning Covid-19 children's book *Juliette and the Mystery Bug*. Terry is a prolific book narrator and host of the popular program *Authors on the Air*. His short stories have been published in several anthologies. He lives and writes on the ocean in Jacksonville, Florida. https://TerryShepherd.com

THE LAUNDRY LARCENY

By ML Condike

I had been living at Sign Point for less than month when things began to disappear. Sign Point is one of those life-plan communities where people "age in place" from the Independent Living apartment building to Assisted Living and, if need be, Memory Care. They also have Skilled Nursing and Rehab for those who need those services temporarily. I'd driven past the complex on Preston Road every day on my way to Southern Methodist University, where I'd worked until retirement.

I'd always admired the community with its stately brick buildings. The original developer had taken care to preserve many of the trees throughout the grounds, giving it a parklike feeling. Ducks, geese, songbirds, and a few squirrels made themselves at home here. So when I retired, moving into the Independent Living building had been an easy choice, especially since I had friends and family at Sign Point too. My bedroom window had a wonderful view of a duck pond. I was admiring it one afternoon when my phone rang. My sister's name appeared on the display.

"Maggie, get over here right away. It's gone," Gracie moaned.

"What's gone?"

"My favorite sky-blue pantsuit." The gossip grapevine had been hot about residents' items going missing, but this was the first time someone I knew was a victim.

"I'll be right over." I grabbed my sweater and dashed to the Assisted Living building next door. Gracie stood in her open doorway as I approached her apartment. I smoothed her thinning white hair that stood up in back where she'd slept on it. Her homemade embroidered shirt—she sewed her own clothes sometimes—hung awry.

"This is horrible," she said.

"I know. Let's go inside and you can give me the scoop." I guided her to the couch. "Go ahead."

"I sent it to the laundry on Tuesday because it had gotten wrinkled and I didn't want them to set in, and now it's gone. When I asked Ruby about it, she said she'd cleaned it and hung it on the delivery rack just before she left for the day. So I should have gotten it yesterday."

"Could she have delivered it to someone else by mistake?"

"No, she said she definitely hadn't seen my pantsuit since she put it on the rack. She hadn't even realized it was missing."

"Does she ever leave the laundry door open?" I wondered if another resident took it. The laundry room was down the hall from Gracie's apartment.

"No. Never."

"Then it has to be an inside job." I thought for a moment. "Who else could get into the laundry?"

"Only people with passkeys. Ruby, obviously, Frank from maintenance, Norman the chaplain, the security guards, and all the attendants."

"That's a lot of people. Are they all trustworthy?"

Gracie thought for a moment. "I'm not sure. Ruby and Frank have been in my place numerous times, and I've never lost a thing. And I'd hate to think the chaplain was a thief."

I remained silent while she considered the honesty of the other employees.

She finally blurted out, "And Elizabeth Brite."

Of course. Sign Point's administrator. She was…not my favorite person.

"Did you notify her about the theft?"

"No. I called you first."

I retrieved my cell phone and called Elizabeth and reported the missing pantsuit. She agreed to meet with me at four o'clock.

Gracie poked me and whispered, "Ask if anyone else has reported missing items."

It seemed I'd be starting our discussion now. I asked Elizabeth the question, then looked at Gracie and shook my head. Before I could say anything more, Elizabeth announced she had a meeting, then immediately disconnected.

"She hung up," I said. "Whew. She gets under my skin."

Gracie laughed. "She can be abrasive. Some residents call her Scotch-Brite behind her back. I bet that's why nobody else has contacted her about any lost items."

"Makes sense."

"Don't worry. You won't see her much. She spends most days schmoozing with Corporate."

"I suspected she was a brownnoser," I said. "Nonetheless, I'll see what I can learn at our meeting. What do you know about the other lost items?"

"There's Phyllis in Skilled Nursing and Carl your SMU friend in Memory Care. They've both had things taken." Both of them? I hadn't heard that. Phyllis, my best friend from high school, was spending a short stay in Skilled Nursing after a nasty fall. She'd move through Rehab, then back to Assisted Living when ready. Carl, a former colleague, lived in the Memory Care building.

"But Phyllis knows of at least four others." Gracie ticked their names off on her fingers. More than one building was involved. Interesting.

"What about Independent Living or Rehab? Any residents in those buildings reported any thefts?" I'd felt safe until now.

"No. But Independent residents don't share our dining room, so I might not hear."

"True. And we do our own laundry in Independent. It's unlikely we would be targeted."

Gracie wrung her hands. "Why my favorite outfit? What can we do?"

"First, let me meet with Elizabeth and see what she thinks. Are you sure you don't want to come with me to the meeting?"

"No. You're much better with things like this."

"Okay. I'll stop by after I see her and let you know her plans."

I kept an open mind as I strolled over to meet with Elizabeth. When I entered the office, her assistant smiled. "Ms. Brite will be right with you."

I could see Elizabeth on the phone. She wore her bleached-blond hair in an updo, exposing her turkey neck. She scowled and waved her skinny arms as she talked. When she disconnected, she stood, straightened her clothes, then came to her door. "Come in."

I followed her into her office, sat in the visitor's chair, and laid out what I knew and my concerns.

Stone-faced, Elizabeth placed her folded hands on the desk. "I appreciate that you let me know about your sister's lost item. We will look into it. But I can't talk about other residents or release the names of people with passkeys. It's a privacy issue."

"It's a security issue, and the residents have a right to know what's going on."

"There's nothing going on. You're the only person who's reported something missing. The pantsuit's probably been misplaced. It'll turn up."

"I told you about the other residents."

She rolled her eyes. "*You* told me. They haven't. It's all unsubstantiated gossip."

I wasn't going to be steamrolled. "Are there other employees besides the obvious who have passkeys?"

"None that you need to know. You're not an employee." She glared at me.

"When we spoke earlier, you gave me the impression you'd be more helpful than this."

"Ms. Miller, I agreed to meet because I wanted to assure you and your sister that you can feel safe here at Sign Point."

"Well, I don't. If you're not going to take this seriously, then I'll investigate the thefts myself."

"You?" She laughed. "What makes you think you can solve a mystery?"

"I've solved more than one during my life," I said.

"Like what?" She raised one eyebrow. "Nothing big, I'm sure."

"I participated on a crime task force at SMU. A black market for math and science books appeared on campus. I went on a stakeout and identified the thieves."

"Humph. This isn't a campus, and we're not dealing with students. We have to be sensitive to the residents' privacy. I don't want you poking around in other people's business." She narrowed her eyes.

"That must be why you haven't called the police."

Elizabeth's face flushed at the mention of law enforcement. "Exactly."

And I'd just caught her in a lie. There had been other thefts reported to her office.

She stood up, put both hands on her desk, and leaned toward me. "I don't want the residents upset. Don't you go poking around and asking questions. Is that clear?"

"Perfectly clear." But that didn't mean I had to do what she said.

Shocked by her attitude, I left her office and walked to Gracie's building, deciding my next course of action would be visiting—and chatting with—my friends. She certainly couldn't object to that. And even if she did, she couldn't stop me.

● ● ●

"She refused to identify others with passkeys," I told Gracie. "And she doesn't want police involvement. It might upset the residents."

"That's no surprise. She's worried about her career. She doesn't care a bit about the residents. But honestly, I'm not crazy about involving the police either." Gracie sighed. "My pantsuit is a small item to Elizabeth, but it was my favorite, and it wasn't cheap. If she refuses to act, then you're our best alternative."

"I'm in." I suspected I'd find a pattern if it was the same perpetrator. "I'll start by chatting with Phyllis and Carl, plus the other residents you mentioned. See what items they lost and when the items went missing. Then I'll interview the staff."

"Ruby and Frank are nice. They won't mind talking to you. I'm not sure about the chaplain, but you can try."

"He's a chaplain. I can't imagine he won't want to help."

● ● ●

I decided to visit Skilled Nursing first and interview Phyllis. I loved her dearly, but I dreaded going in there. Not because I didn't care about the people. Because I cared too much. Walking into the common area tore at my heartstrings.

Nurses wheeled a dozen patients into the open area each day to provide a change of scenery. The residents reminded me of nesting baby birds, their beaks wide open, pointing up, when the mother bird arrived with a worm. Here all heads turned toward the opened door whenever anyone arrived, their eyes hungry for a visitor, any visitor, family, friend, or stranger. I couldn't visit all of them. I smiled, waved, and went directly to Phyllis's room.

"Maggie! What brings you here today?" Phyllis swung her boney legs off the bed, righted herself, then straightened her flowered smock to cover her knobby knees.

"Why you, of course. And the case of the missing items."

Phyllis rolls her eyes. "How did you hear about that?"

I sat in her bedside visitor's chair. "Grapevine and Gracie. She lost a pantsuit. But she didn't know the details of your theft."

"Honestly. I can't believe someone stole my favorite satin nightgown—the fuchsia one!"

"A nightgown? When did you notice it missing?" I'd expected glasses, jewelry, books, or something more valuable.

"My best one. I'd just gotten my weekly laundry back, but I didn't want to wait on the nightgown because I'd spilled coffee on it."

"What day was that?"

"Tuesday."

The same day Gracie's pantsuit disappeared.

"You can imagine my surprise when Ruby didn't return it the next day," Phyllis twisted a cotton embroidered handkerchief as she relived the experience. "She's always so efficient."

"You were here all day?"

"Yep. I spent the afternoon binge-watching Hallmark movies." She smiled. "I know. They're predictable. But at my age, surprises could kill me."

I hugged Phyllis before I left.

On my way back to Gracie's I pondered the case. Ruby could be the thief even though she seems honest, I reasoned. The pantsuit and the nightgown were both nice items. Could Ruby be selling them at a consignment shop?

Back at Gracie's I shared what I'd learned. "Do you think Ruby has money troubles?"

"I have no idea. But truthfully, we've never discussed personal issues. We always talk about laundry and clothing. Did you talk to Carl?"

"Not yet." I hadn't yet visited Carl since I moved into Sign Point. He'd gone to high school with Gracie and worked with me for quite a few years in the History Department at SMU.

"He won't be much help, considering…" Gracie shook her head. "Such a sad story."

Carl had been a fellow professor until he had a terrible bicycle accident while on a trip to Egypt a few years ago. A head injury put him in a coma. When he awoke, he thought he was Xerxes the Great, a king of the Achaemenid Empire.

"I'll never forget his first class when he returned to teaching," I said. "He strolled into his class dressed like a Persian king and claimed he was Xerxes. He created an uproar. We all thought he was acting."

He never regained his memory. Not long after, his family moved him into Assisted Living here.

"He was so confused those first few months," Gracie said.

"I lost track of him after he left SMU," I said. "How did he end up in Memory Care? I'd heard he was doing pretty well in Assisted Living."

"At first, he had good days and bad days. Then bad days outweighed the good. He became convinced a young attendant was his wife, Esther. You know, the Jewish queen in the Bible who kept her faith a secret from Xerxes because the king had ordered all Jews killed."

"Did Carl get violent?" He'd been such a sweet and gentle person at SMU.

"No. But the attendant had to leave her job because he followed her everywhere. That's when they put him in Memory Care. He's been there for most of his stay. But I get to see him regularly. Raymond, an attendant, asked for volunteers who knew Carl before his injury to attend supervised visits by the pool. A few of us try to make it at least once a week. At times

Carl seems to know me." Gracie paused. "At least, I like to think he does."

"I should have gone to see him before now," I said. "It's time to correct that problem."

"Tomorrow. You'll need to do it tomorrow. He doesn't do so well later in the day."

Ahh. So sad.

First thing the next morning, I walked over Memory Care to visit Carl. The lobby desk faced the front doors. I waved and displayed my ID card, and the desk clerk unlocked the door. After a brief conversation and a phone call, a stocky middle-aged male attendant appeared.

"Raymond, I assume." I reached out my hand.

We shook hands. "You must be Maggie. Follow me. Carl's having a good day."

A window in Carl's small second-story room faced a neighboring medical complex. Carl stood staring out. He wore a white terry robe. He'd stuffed his right arm in the sleeve, but his left arm and shoulder remained bare, showing off a smattering of freckles. He'd wrapped the empty sleeve around his middle and tied it with the sash, so it didn't hang.

"Carl, you have a visitor," Raymond said.

Carl turned and blushed when he saw me. "Maggie. It's been a long time." His homemade paper sandals scuffed as he walked toward me. "I'm sorry to be dressed this way, but my robe and sandals have gone missing."

Raymond's surprised face told it all. "He knows you."

I smiled back at Carl. "I didn't come here to visit your clothes. How have you been?"

"Fine except for the thievery. Come sit down." We did, and I said, "What can you tell me about them going missing?"

"It's the strangest thing. I spilled goat stew on my robe, so obviously, being king, I couldn't wear it soiled."

"Obviously."

"I returned to my room after lunch, put on this dreadful rag, and sent Raymond to my laundress with my royal robe."

Awed by his total emersion in his new identity, I said, "Go on."

"I've not seen it since."

"When did this happen?"

"I think it was in four hundred eighty BC."

I bit my lip. "I mean what time?"

"Oh…time…time. Let me think." Carl tapped his chin with his index finger. "It had to be around two p.m."

"Which day?"

"I don't know."

"It doesn't matter. What's important is you remembered me and know your royal robe is missing." I smiled at Raymond. ""Do you know which day it was?"

"It was Tuesday. I always take his clothes to the laundry Tuesday afternoon, so the robe went on top of the pile."

I nodded. The same day Gracie's and Phyllis's clothing went missing. A pattern!

He winked at me then put his hand on Carl's shoulder. "Your Majesty, how is it you know Maggie?"

Carl grinned. "She's Esther's favorite servant. I'd never forget her face."

"I'm honored." I bowed my head as I spoke.

Carl and I visited for a half hour before he tired from his effort to be social.

"What do you say, Carl? Ready for a nap?" Raymond asked.

"Yes. Matters of court wear me out." Carl curled into a fetal position on his bed and Raymond draped him with a blanket.

"I'll find my way out," I said to Raymond, then turned to Carl. "Thank you, Your Majesty. It's been a wonderful visit."

"It has," Carl mumbled.

So now I knew Carl had lost his kingly robes and sandals along with his grasp of reality. I wanted to be sad, but the truth was, Carl seemed happy. He really believed he was Xerxes.

As I left Carl's I revisited my consignment idea. It seemed highly unlikely someone would try to sell a robe and used sandals, so there must be another reason those clothing items disappeared. Plus, all the items were at the laundry on Tuesday. Could Ruby have ruined them in the wash and was ashamed to admit it?

My phone vibrated in my pocket as I walked across the compound toward my unit. It was Gracie again. "Hey. What's up?"

"You've got to come here right away!"

Gracie's shrilled voice sent goose bumps up my arms.

"Run if you can. It's an emergency." Gracie disconnected.

I hustled, a sort of walk-run, to Gracie's unit and when I arrived, I could see the excitement wasn't at her place. "What's going on?"

Gracie grabbed my arm. "It's awful."

"What happened?"

"I'd just drifted off for a nap when I heard Ruby screaming. So, I ran to my door,"

"And?"

"Ruby was standing in the laundry doorway, holding up my sky-blue pantsuit. And it was covered in blood."

"Are you sure it was blood?"

"It looked like blood."

Just then Ruby and a security guard stepped from the laundry room into the hallway. The guard held a phone to his ear. "Yes. Foul play. We need the police here right away."

Well, at least they'll call the police about some things.

Ruby stood, wiping her doe-like eyes, then slipped the tissue into her apron pocket.

Gracie rushed over. "Ruby, what happened? Was that blood on my pantsuit?"

"Your pantsuit got the better end of the deal," Ruby said. "Scotch-Brite's folded up in a laundry bin under a load of sheets. Dead! And she's wearing Phyllis's fuchsia nightgown."

Although not crazy about Elizabeth, I felt terrible about her death.

Gracie began to cry, so I guided her back into her unit. I told her about my meeting with Carl, trying to distract her. When I'd answered all her questions, I said, "I'm going down the hall, see if I can find out more about what's happening."

Before I could ask any questions, the police arrived and shooed everyone back into their units. I joined Gracie in hers. "If I stay with you, I can listen by the door."

I pulled a chair to Gracie's partially opened door, sat, and surveilled the laundry room.

After nearly an hour of watching police go in and out of the laundry room, I hadn't learned anything useful. Then an officer spotted me. "Is this your apartment?"

"No. It's my sister's, but I live at Sign Point too. She's extremely upset. Ruby found her pantsuit in the bin with the body."

The officer shook his head. "You better scoot back to your own place. We'll chat with you later." He handed me a pad where he'd been collecting names, units, and phone numbers. While adding my name to his list, a police officer rolled out a bin from the laundry room. It was clearly marked "Memory Care – 2nd Floor."

Elizabeth must have been murdered in Memory Care, then moved to Assisted Living. Why would the killer do that? And who was it? It had to be someone who could move a bin without attracting attention.

I returned the officer's notepad. After he walked off, I said to Gracie, "That bin was from Carl's building. Someone who works there must be involved. What do you know about Raymond?" I hated mentioning him by name, but he was the only Memory Care attendant I knew.

"I can't imagine it was him. Raymond's a gentle soul. Look at how he handles Carl," Gracie said.

"You're right. I doubt it's him." But I wasn't ready to eliminate him as a suspect.

Ruby knocked on the open door, then scurried inside Gracie's apartment and shut the door. "Sorry to intrude, but I overheard your conversation. Talk to Frank in maintenance. He saw Elizabeth in Memory Care Tuesday night. He may know something."

The same day Gracie's and Phyllis's clothes went to the laundry.

"What would she be doing there at night?" I asked.

Ruby shrugged. "The police asked me the same thing when I told them what Frank saw."

I hadn't kept tabs on Elizabeth, but in my short time living here, I'd never seen her at the complex after business hours.

Between her being at Memory Care the night of the thefts and ending up dead in a Memory Care bin today—the morning after I reported the thefts—something was definitely fishy in that building.

Before leaving Gracie's, I asked Ruby what she knew about the missing clothing and if she had any idea who might have stolen the garments. She claimed ignorance, just like she knew nothing about Elizabeth's murder. She seemed believable, so I decided to move on to Frank.

The maintenance building sat out of view behind Memory Care. It held lawn equipment, tools, replacement parts for small repairs like faucets, blinds, and doors. Frank was loading blinds into a cart when I arrived.

"Frank." I waved and rushed over. "Do you have a minute to talk? Ruby said you saw Elizabeth in Memory Care Tuesday night."

His curly black hair rested on the shoulders of his gray coveralls. It swung out from under his baseball cap when he looked around. "I did. I've already told the police what I know."

"I understand, but I'm doing a little investigating on my own. My sister, Gracie, had clothes stolen that ended up in the laundry bin from Memory Care with Elizabeth. I'm trying to figure out how her clothes got there and why Elizabeth was in the building Tuesday night."

"Don't know, but that's not all they found."

"What do you mean?"

"A lot of people have been losing items lately. I hear King Xerxes's bloody robe had been tossed on top of Scotch-Brite."

My heart stopped. "Please don't tell me Carl did this. He didn't seem violent. He even knew me after three years."

"I didn't say he did it. I said his missing robe was in the laundry bin. But that's not all." Frank whispered, "Scotch-Brite was wearing a purple nightgown."

"Don't you have work to do, Frank?" a baritone voice said.

I turned to see Norman, the in-residence chaplain, walking toward us. Perfect. He was one of the other people I needed to interview.

"Yes, sir." Frank gave me a sideways glance, then hopped on the tractor and drove toward the Independent Living building.

"Maggie," Norman said, adjusting his eyeglasses, "did I hear you talking with Frank about the missing clothing?"

A perfect opening. "Yes, I—"

"I thought Elizabeth Brite asked you not to bother people about this."

Busted.

"I couldn't help myself. Gracie's beside herself. Her favorite pantsuit was stolen and is part of the crime scene. I decided to check around to see how it could have gotten in the bin with Elizabeth. You wouldn't know anything about that, would you?"

Norman frowned. "No, I don't. I understand your interest, but it's not a good idea to poke your nose into police matters. I suggest you return to your unit and let the authorities handle this."

Had Norman actually told me to go home, as if I were a child? Well, it seemed there was no use in trying to ask him any more questions. "Yes. Of course. I'm on my way."

I mulled over the murder all the way back to my place. Something happened in the Memory Care facility resulting in Elizabeth's death. It was the perfect location for a murder. None of the residents were reliable witnesses. But why would Elizabeth visit there at night?

The next morning, I took Phyllis out for a spin in her wheelchair around the complex. Gracie and three of her sewing buddies joined us. We landed outside Memory Care—and not by chance. I'd purposefully guided us there. The police were prohibiting everyone except building residents and staff from entering, but nothing prevented us from sitting on the benches in front.

Word was that the police had concluded Elizabeth died in Memory Care, as I'd suspected. They'd yet to discover the scene of the crime.

I watched as a group of officers stood outside the front door talking. "We might learn more about Elizabeth's death by hanging around here. Perfect surveillance location. Police are constantly streaming in and out of the building."

Gracie started fiddling with her ears. "Darn."

"What's the matter?" I asked.

"I can't hear them. Even with my hearing aids turned up to full volume."

"I don't think they're made for surveillance," I said.

Frank and Ruby joined us, Frank looking my way. "Anything new?"

I shook my head. "Wish I could look around inside." I eyed Ruby as I spoke, but she didn't seem bothered at all.

"Not much to see in there," Frank said. "Private and semi-private rooms. A playroom similar to the one in Rehab with a kitchen area, crafts, exercise equipment, and a Ping-Pong table."

Eyes wide, a tiny lady from Gracie's sewing group asked, "Do you think she was killed on the Ping-Pong table?"

"Probably not," Ruby said. "She was covered in blood from a head wound. The police would have noticed it on the table."

A head wound. Had someone snuck up on her from behind?

"I'd sure love to visit Carl," I said. And maybe chat Raymond up some more too. "He's in Memory Care."

"Who is Carl?" the same sewing lady asked, lifting her eyebrows toward her white hairline.

"You might know him as Xerxes."

"Oh, my dear, you mean the king. He's so handsome. And that exquisite embroidered velvet robe. So terrible it was ruined."

We sat in silence for few minutes. Ruby and Frank moved a few feet away while Frank smoked a cigarette.

I wished I could think of ways to jog Carl's memory. He might have seen something.

Gracie broke the silence. "I have an idea."

"Spill." I'd run flat out of ideas. Maybe Gracie had an epiphany.

"We can sew Xerxes a new royal robe. Remember those lamé curtains from Hazel's apartment? They're still in the sewing closet." She stood with her arms raised to the heavens.

"Curtains?" *Nope, not an epiphany.*

"Perfect! Let's go right now," the little white-haired lady said, ignoring my disbelief.

"I'm staying here a little longer with Frank and Ruby." I decided not to spoil Gracie's enlightenment—curtains for Pete's sake. "Have fun."

"I'm staying with Maggie," Phyllis said.

Gracie and her sewing buddies waddled off like a gaggle of geese, while Frank and Ruby came back over. Frank had finished his cigarette.

"You sure neither of you know any more about the stolen clothes or Elizabeth's death or why she would have been in Memory Care last Tuesday night?" I asked.

Frank looked like he'd swallowed a canary. He knew something.

But it was Ruby who spoke first. "I guess there's no reason to keep this a secret, now that she's gone. I guess we should've told the cops. She'd went into the hidden room."

"The what?"

"It's on the second floor. Chaplain Norman uses it for…"

Ruby stopped and looked at Frank.

Frank's neck turned bright red. "For personal recreation."

"What kind of personal recreation?" Phyllis asked.

Sweat formed on Frank's forehead. He wiped it off with his sleeve. "Personal personal."

What did that mean? "Have you been in the room?" I asked.

Frank shook his head. "No, ma'am. Never. It doesn't open with a key."

"How does it open?" Phyllis asked. "Is it a magic door?"

"No," Frank and Ruby said in unison.

"It's at the back of the utility closet at the end of the far hall, right by your friend Carl's room," Frank said. "But we couldn't figure out how to open it. There's no knob."

"Tell her." Ruby slapped Frank's back. "Spit it out. Tell her what you told me."

"Chaplain Norman and Scotch-Brite are the only ones who know how to enter the room."

I laughed. "You think it was that kind of personal recreation? Scotch-Brite and the chaplain! No way."

Frank's cheeks flushed. "That's where I saw her Tuesday night, entering that closet. I was leaving Xerxes's room after unplugging his toilet."

"Maybe they're the ones who've been stealing all the stuff." Phyllis glanced down at herself, then looked at me. "She and I are about the same size."

"Look," Frank said. "The police are leaving."

We watched as the last of Dallas's finest marched down to their squad cars and drove off.

"I'm going inside to see if I can visit Carl. Maybe I can sneak a look at that hidden door." I turned to Ruby. "Will you take Phyllis back to her room for me when she's ready?"

"Of course."

"Great. Thank you." I turned to Phyllis before leaving. "Sorry I can't stay. See you later."

The same clerk manned the desk in the Memory Care lobby. "Hi again. Have the police removed the building's lockdown? I'd love to visit my friend Carl."

The clerk laughed. "They gave up interviewing before they finished the second floor. You wouldn't believe the stories! Everything from a hostile takeover to a conspiracy theory."

Carl's attendant, Raymond, appeared and waved me through.

"Have you heard anything new about the missing clothing or what happened here?" I asked as we walked toward Carl's room.

"No. I wish I did."

I nodded. "How's Carl doing?"

"He's settling down. Losing his royal robes really upset him." Raymond sighed. "He was doing so well until that disaster."

We entered Carl's room and found him laying on the bed with a pillow over his eyes.

Raymond touched Carl's arm. "Carl… Your Highness. You have a visitor."

Carl removed the pillow and looked at me. "Concubine, what brings you here? Has something happened to the queen?"

My neck heated. "The…queen and I are fine." I looked toward the attendant. "Raymond, no need for you to stick around."

He shrugged. "I'm happy to stay. He might need me."

"Okay." I hoped Raymond wasn't involved. I preferred to talk to Carl alone, but apparently, he wasn't going anywhere. "My king, much has been amiss in the castle. Perchance, have you seen any foul play?"

"Foul play?" Carl sat up. "Foul play is all I see. Night after night it goes on until…"

"Until what?" Goose bumps formed on my arms.

"It happened at the full moon—two nights ago. My queen and that villainous holy man."

"What about them?" the attendant asked.

"It never stops. The music. The walls are alive."

"What are you talking about?" Raymond put his arm around Carl's shoulder.

"Weeks it's gone on." Carl covered his ears and rocked his body. "I thought I would go mad. I did go mad."

Raymond's gaze flicked to me for a second before returning to Carl. "What do you mean you went mad?"

"I followed them to the tunnel and watched as they disappeared into the wall." Carl rocked with more force. "I returned to my chamber, where I heard the moaning and laughter again behind the wall. Then came a scream. I knew then that Rashnu, god of the dead, had passed his judgment."

Had he heard a scream of pain or ecstasy? Had he heard the murder being committed or had he later committed it himself in anger over the noise?

"What did you do?" I asked, fearing the worst.

Raymond's face paled, but he stood by Carl.

"I prayed to Ahura Mazda, king of the gods, asking him to release me from my penance."

His penance? I stared at Carl, and beneath his anguish, I could still see my sweet, kind friend. How could I even think that he might have killed Elizabeth? I turned to Raymond. "He didn't do it."

Raymond nodded and rubbed Carl's back.

Looking exhausted, Carl ceased rocking and collapsed on his bed. Raymond covered him with a blanket.

"Can you show me the utility closet?" I asked Raymond.

"Sure. This way."

We went into the hall. The closet was literally next door. Raymond opened it. From what I could see, mostly empty shelves covered the entire rear wall. "I need a closer look. Is there a light?"

The attendant found a switch inside and flicked it on.

"Look at this. It's a Murphy door." I'd seen one in an old movie. "The bookcase is actually a door on a hinge. We should be able to push it open."

I tried the right side first, pressing on the shelves. "Ninety percent of the people in the world are right-handed. Maybe the builder was too."

No luck.

Then I tried the left side. It budged, but it was too heavy. I couldn't move it by myself.

"Let me try." Raymond put his weight into it, and the heavy door opened, revealing a pitch-black room. He found a switch and turned on the lights.

"Holy mother of Jupiter." I couldn't believe my eyes.

"What the heck?" Raymond said.

The room was the size of a typical two-person hospital room, except for the small part carved out for the utility closet. It was a love nest of sorts. It contained a bed, a small trampoline, whips, vases full of large feathers, and a statue of Eros.

Blood covered the floor next to the trampoline. Someone had tried to clean it up and managed to smear it all over. A pile of unsorted items covered the top of a vanity. Costumes, including a clown suit, a tutu with pink pointe slippers, and a lion's suit, lined an entire wall. Plus, a bunny suit hung from a light fixture over the bed.

I dialed 911. "This is Maggie Miller at Sign Point. May I speak to the officer in charge of the murder investigation here? It's important."

I was transferred and soon a man said, "This is Detective Hernandez."

"I'm Maggie Miller, a resident at Sign Point. We've found the scene of the murder."

"Where?" he asked.

"In Memory Care's second-floor utility closet. It's in the back hall. You'll have to see it to believe it.

"Don't touch a thing. I'll be right there." He disconnected.

"He said don't touch anything," I shouted, but Raymond had already wandered inside and was leafing through a book. He turned it so I could read the title: *Sexual Deviance* by D. Richard Laws. Then he opened to a page with a picture that I'll not forget for the rest of my life.

In shock and awe, we both backed out of the room.

"What in heaven's name were they up to in that dreadful room?" Gracie asked when I told her who the thieves were and where the clothes had been stashed.

"Foreplay, I'd guess." I shuddered, recalling the picture branded on my brain. Then I told Gracie everything I knew.

Later we learned that the police found Elizabeth's and Norman's fingerprints all over the room. Norman's handprint was in the blood where he'd tried to clean it up. They also found a video of Elizabeth wearing Gracie's pantsuit and a white wig while she jumped on the trampoline and Norman tickled her with feathers.

Of all the reasons I'd theorized for the stolen clothing, I'd never imagined the actual one.

I was happy that neither Ruby nor Raymond had been responsible for Elizabeth's death. They both seemed so nice, I'd hated suspecting them.

The police recovered all of the residents' missing items. Once confronted, the chaplain admitted Elizabeth told him about the room recently, and they'd decided to use it for their liaisons, playing games and…doing other things. For thrills, they'd steal items to use while in there.

Norman swore Elizabeth died from an accident. He claimed she got excited and jumped so high that her head hit the ceiling fan and tumbled off the trampoline. That's when she broke her neck and fractured her skull on the wing of Eros.

When asked why he tried to cover it up, he said, "to preserve her dignity."

I'm still happy with my decision to move to Sign Point. We have a new administrator now. Her name is Fern. All of us love her.

Gracie and her sewing group made Xerxes a linen robe from the discarded curtains. I accompanied them when they delivered it to Carl. He and I had developed a bond—well maybe a sycophantic relationship. I pretend to be a concubine and fawn over him, and he blossoms with the attention. I am now an expert in ancient Persian history and sympathetic to Xerxes's distress over his vilification by Alexander the Great.

"Nice! The colors accent your hazel eyes," I said as Carl appeared wearing his new gold robe.

"And look at these." Carl stuck out a foot, showing off new lace-up sandals. "My court subjects have provided my footwear."

Gracie raised her eyebrows. "Court subjects?"

Raymond leaned toward me. "We visit Dallas Hall on the SMU campus monthly to meet with a few of his former colleagues from the History Department. He's convinced it's the palace."

"They're my former colleagues too. I'll have to accompany you sometime."

Carl looked around and spotted his attendant. "Manservant. Please lace my sandals."

I leaned down, saying, "I'll do it." Considering how Carl had helped uncover the secrets behind the thefts and Elizabeth's death, it was the least I could do for my king.

ML (MARY LOU) CONDIKE'S professional career included computer science, industrial management, and small-business ownership. Once retired, she completed the Southern Methodist University Writer's Path. Her stories appear in anthologies *Strange & Sweet*, *Tall Tales and Timeless Stories*, *Malice in Dallas*, and *More Words from the End of the Road*. Her first novel, *The Desk from Hoboken*, is with an agent. Notable awards include first place in the fifteenth annual Writer's Digest Popular Fiction Awards in the Mystery/Crime category and second place in the Tennessee Williams Short Story Contest. She's a member of Mystery Writers of America, Sisters in Crime, Granbury Writers' Bloc, and Key West Writers Guild. https://mlcondike.com

WHO SHOT THE PARTY CRASHER?

By Amber Royer

We breezed into Dallas in a rented Gulf Stream Coach RV. It really had sleeping room for five, but there were six of us, and we were making due. Which meant, as the only non-senior citizen, I'd had a sleeping bag on the floor. The RV model was called a Conquest, and Aunt Brenda couldn't say it without giggling. I was supposed to be the immature one, in my thirties and unemployed between singing gigs, but my aunt had been cracking off-color jokes ever since she and her friends from the retirement condos in Florida had piled into the vehicle. There had been no discussion of who would sit where. Annamaria—a former bank manager with dyed golden brown hair, subdued makeup, and an addiction to mom jeans—had gotten behind the wheel at the start of the trip. And the rest of us had fallen in line, with me opposite my aunt at the tiny dining table.

"Conquest," Brenda said again, out of the blue, as we turned in to the Whataburger parking lot. She patted her short curly gray hair and made goo-goo eyes at everybody. They all started laughing—though I think half of them were just humoring her—until one wheel of the RV hit the curb with an uncomfortable jolt.

Priya let out a squeak and reached out to steady herself against the RV's refrigerator as she almost fell. She was a retired anesthesiologist with glossy black hair that looked natural. The cheap tortoiseshell frames on her glasses counterpointed the elegance of her pink silk blouse, and flowing floral scarf. I'd never seen her without some kind of scarf and a wrist full of bangle bracelets, and today was no exception, even though it has just been us in the RV the whole trip. She opened the fridge door to take out a bottle of water. "Are you sure we have to stop for fast food?" Gesturing to the two-burner stove, she added, "I could just make us something to eat. I could do masala dosas. You always like those on rummy night."

Annamaria said, "We're stopping at this Whataburger. It's the one thing Gerta asked for when we planned this trip. Though why this specific one, I have no idea."

Not that Gerta was explaining now. Somehow Gerta—a former restaurant owner who had turned her Dallas eatery's keys over to her daughter less than six months ago—had managed to sleep through all of this. I suspected she took something for motion sickness or maybe a sleeping pill. Part of the point of taking a road trip is spending time with the people you are traveling with. But maybe Gerta didn't feel the same way. Or maybe she was regretting the whole retire-and-move-to-Florida thing.

But Whataburger? Why would a chef want fast food? It was puzzling. But I wasn't going to be the one to wake her up and ask. I was going to be traveling with them in this RV for the next five days. And Gerta had already criticized my posture—which comes from the fact I hate being tall—and said my sweater looked like it came from a thrift store. Which it had, but she said it as if I was a step away from living on the streets, even though I'd paired the purple wool with the luxe leather jacket I always wear, a holdover signature look from the days when my band's success made me famous. And then Gerta had offered me a job at her former restaurant. She had been genuinely trying to be nice. Oh, how the mighty have fallen, but I'm not that desperate. Yet.

The last of the Ah-ah-ahs, as they called themselves since their names all ended in *a*, was Lydia. She was stick thin and wore ancient band tees every day with leather pants. I felt a kinship with her, since she looked like she could have been part of the music scene. Amazingly, she was the quiet one, sitting on the little sofa, crocheting.

Actually, they kept trying to make me the last Ah-ah-ah. They'd dubbed me an honorary member of their group, since my name ended in an *a* too. But I have a hard time wanting to be part of anything, after what had happened with my band.

As she tucked her crochet into her oversized bag, Lydia asked, "What's a Whataburger?"

I knew Lydia hadn't been listening to Annamaria and all the planning chatter. Another reason why it felt like she could have been part of my former life. "It's a Texas thing," I said. "Texans who move away dream about their burgers—even though it's fast food." I had grown up in North Texas, so I was no exception. I'd actually gotten my mom to FedEx me one once, when I'd been on the road with my band. "Try the spicy ketchup."

Lydia gave me a skeptical look. She'd never been to Texas before, had moved to Florida from New York. I shrugged, then looked back at Gerta, who was still snoring softly.

"What should we do about her?" I asked.

Priya shook Gerta's shoulder. "Hey, Gerta, we're at the burger place you wanted."

Without opening her eyes, Gerta murmured, "I need a Whatachick'n and fries." There was a long pause, then she waved a hand and said, "I always used to come here with my sister." She had on a fancy diving watch, which I hadn't noticed her wearing before.

Priya returned to the front of the RV and said softly, "I'll get her order and bring it back out here. It's so sad her sister died. Maybe she thought it would be therapeutic to come here, but now she's just depressed."

Annamaria pulled us slowly through the parking lot, circling the building. "Hear that? I think we have a flat." She sighed and finally stopped. "We might as well go inside. I'll call AAA from there."

We spent a long time at Whataburger, waiting for AAA to text they were on their way. Finally, they came, changed the tire, and left. The road trip could continue!

We all got ready to pile back into the RV, with Aunt Brenda leading the way, until she stopped with her rear end sticking out of the door. "Oh, dear," she said loudly.

"What happened?" I asked.

"Look for yourself." Aunt Brenda backed out of the doorway.

I stepped up into the RV. There, sprawled on the floor, was a guy about my age wearing an old-fashioned suit with a wide striped tie—with a bullet hole in him. Blood had seeped out onto his white shirt. There was a cowboy hat half-on, half-off his head. You don't actually see that many cowboy hats in North Dallas. Especially not ones with elaborate feathered hatbands. I stared at him, stunned. When I could speak, I asked, "Why does he look familiar?"

From the doorway Brenda said, "Because he's dressed like the character who got shot on *Dallas*."

I blinked, trying to process this. "As in the show from with the place we came here to see? That's a weird coincidence."

We'd come to Texas to visit Southfork Ranch, the set of the long-running soap opera these ladies had loved back in the eighties. You could still tour it—though I'd never had a desire to when I'd lived here. I'd watched a couple of episodes of the soap just to have some clue when we got there. It was…really dramatic. The sensibility seemed to capture the late seventies and early eighties perfectly.

But this guy was too young to have been a fan of the show. So why was he dressed in costume-party clothes that were decades out of date? And more important, why was he dead inside our RV?

I stepped outside, Annamaria peered in, and in seconds had dialed 911. Into her phone, she said, "I don't know. He could have been there when AAA changed our tire. They didn't go inside. There certainly wasn't a body in the RV when we got out of it."

Meanwhile, the other ladies all took turns peering into the RV. When Priya had her turn, she gasped and dropped the bag containing Gerta's lunch. "That's Vinnie Explores. My granddaughter loves his YouTube channel. He goes to different places and takes travel and food videos. He's known for crashing parties and events and then filming people until somebody kicks him out—though sometimes the host is flattered instead." She looked back inside. "He won't be crashing anymore family fiestas."

Lydia stepped into the RV and then came back holding a phone.

"Hey!" Annamaria said, having just ended her call. "Is that his? It's evidence. You shouldn't have touched it."

"Too late now," Lydia said. "He had it unlocked, probably so he could access his camera feed. It seems to be pulling video from a camera somewhere on his body. Right now it's showing the ceiling of our RV. Recognize that light fixture?" She held up the phone so we could see the screen.

I nodded. "Can you go back a bit? Maybe the camera captured who shot him."

Lydia started tapping the phone, with us watching over her shoulders. Eventually she got to the point where Vinnie entered the unlocked RV, after we left for lunch. Annamaria had left the

key with Gerta so she could lock it if she came inside, so Vinnie
had been able to walk right in, straight to Gerta. He shook her
awake. Clearly, she knew him. They talked about him going with
them to Southfork to film the tour for his show. Vinnie turned to
get Gerta a drink from the fridge, and in the corner of the frame,
a gloved hand was reaching into the RV's door with a gun. There
was a bang, and Vinnie fell. The rest of it was unclear from the
angle of the footage, but the audio was straightforward enough:
someone with a muffled voice forced Gerta to leave with them.

We all stared at each other, shocked. How could we not have
noticed that Gerta wasn't in the RV? We all took another look
inside to verify this fact, and Annamaria even checked the
bathroom and the closet, stepping carefully over poor Vinnie.
Still no Gerta.

Aunt Brenda said, "This is more of a mystery even then
when we were all trying to figure out who shot J.R."

The other Ah-ah-ahs all nodded sagely. They didn't really
have that much in common, aside from age and a shared
connection with a soap opera that they still cared about, even
though it had been off the air for decades. That just goes to show
about the power of story.

Annamaria said, "But it's a mystery for the police to figure
out, not us."

Aunt Brenda said, "If we wait around for the police,
something might happen to Gerta."

Priya said, "It's probably already too late. If something is
going to happen, it's happened."

Lydia said nothing, just looked distraught.

But then they all looked at me. And Aunt Brenda said,
"What do you think, Manda?"

Sure. Bring me into this. Just because I'd been through all of
this before, when I was twelve and my dad disappeared. Growing
up without him had been hard. He'd been the one who'd always
encouraged me, and spent time on trail rides with me, and got me

into barrel racing to keep me from getting into too much trouble. The emptiness of him being gone never left my family. No one's family should have to go through that.

I took the dead man's phone and held it up. "We have to at least try." Though I wasn't sure how we were going to do that. We had no idea which direction Vinnie's killer had gone and no signs of Gerta.

I fumbled the phone, and when I picked it up—terrified it had broken on the pavement—the screen had gone back a menu. There was more than one camera. I clicked over to the other feed, and I was looking at a pair of scarred, age-spotted hands, folded gently in a lap. They were chef's hands, accented with a precision diving watch. It was Gerta. The camera was on her somewhere. She must have gotten it from Vinnie, as part of whatever they had been planning on filming at Southfork. Maybe the watch had been part of the plan too, allowing for split-second timing. She shifted, straightening up—regaining the perfect posture she had modeled for me—and the camera showed the dash of the car she was sitting in. I could see out the window, and as they passed streets, I caught a glimpse of a sculpture.

"I recognize that," I said. "They're driving past the big eyeball downtown. They're heading north through Dallas."

"They haven't gotten far," Aunt Brenda said. "We could catch up."

"Oh no," Annamaria said. "The police are on their way. We are not driving off with the corpse of that nice young man."

"Maybe we can call an Uber," Priya said.

"There's no time," I said. "Maybe I can go in Whataburger and see if anyone will let us borrow a car."

"Or we can just borrow one," Lydia said. She opened the case she kept her crochet needles in and pulled out a flexible flat piece of metal. I spied a set of lockpicks in there too.

"Can we actually do that?" I squeaked.

"No, we can't," Annamaria said. "That's illegal."

"But Gerta's in danger," I justified. "Who knows how long it will take the police to find them? Yet we can literally follow that car right now."

Lydia nipped over to a bright-red classic car, easily big enough for us to all fit on its rolled leather seats. Before I knew it, she'd popped the door open.

"Older cars are easier to start," she said with a shrug.

I stared at Lydia. Who was this woman, before she wound up at that retirement community? Not a drummer, as I'd half assumed.

Annamaria didn't seem happy about it, but she slid into the driver's seat after Lydia got the car started. "If we're doing this, I'm driving. I don't trust any of you old birds behind the wheel." She looked at me. "And I don't really know you."

I guessed I didn't come across as the most responsible person, given my between-jobs state. "Fair point." I piled into the back seat with Priya and Aunt Brenda, balancing both Vinnie's phone and my own phone on my lap.

As we drove out of the lot. I used the camera feed on Vinnie's phone to track Gerta's progress past street signs, and my own phone to look up information.

"This is all so odd," Priya said. "Who kidnaps someone out of an RV?"

"This could be about Gerta," Lydia pointed out. "She was from this area, and she still has some connections here. She told me her nephew still lives in this area."

"Maybe that nephew was Vinnie," I said, Googling Gerta's name and Vinnie's. Lo and behold I found a photo that clearly had both of them in it, from an event honoring Gerta's restaurant. And, yes! It mentioned that Vinnie was indeed Gerta's nephew. There was a girl in the photo, clinging to Vinnie's arm. Pointing to the screen, I nudged Priya and asked, "Know who that is?"

"That's Sapphire Eats," she said.

"Don't any of these people have real names?" Aunt Brenda asked.

"I'm sure they do," Priya said, "but what fun would that be?"

There was a guy in the picture on the other side of Sapphire Eats. "Who's that?"

Priya squinted at the image. "That's Vinnie's brother Ben. Must be an old photo. They don't talk anymore, because Ben stole Sapphire from Vinnie. And then Sapphire broke up with Ben too."

That's a lot of gossip. Sounded like Priya liked Vinnie's YouTube videos as much as her granddaughter did.

Priya gestured at the edge of the screen. "I think that half face in the corner of the image is another restaurant owner. Vinnie crashed a party being held at that man's place, and it got ugly."

The car in the video feed passed another landmark—this time the base of Reunion Tower—before taking a turn and heading out of town, toward one of the rural areas in the Metroplex. "Turn here," I told Annamaria. "I think we can catch up some time."

A lot of people probably had motive to murder Vinnie, given his YouTubing. But which one of them would have wanted to kidnap Gerta? Or maybe the killer hadn't expected anyone to be in the RV and hadn't been able to bring themselves to kill an old lady, even if she had been a witness. Although, in that case, what did they plan to do with Gerta? Either way, the danger of the killer getting up the nerve to silence Gerta was real.

Out of nowhere, Priya said, "I think she's been drugged."

"Pardon?" Aunt Brenda asked.

"Gerta," Priya said. "She slept all day. That's not like her. At first, I thought she took something for motion sickness, but the more I remember how deeply she was sleeping, I think she was drugged, that someone intended to kidnap her. But I'm not sure how."

I shuddered. "Are you suggesting that someone has been following us? That's impossible. They would have had to have been on the road behind us since we left Florida."

Priya shrugged. "Creepy, I know. But I don't know what else to think."

Priya used to be an anesthesiologist, so it was probably best to trust her judgment about such things. But didn't that mean that Gerta was the intended victim of this crime? That what happened to Vinnie could have just been wrong-place-wrong-time? Maybe I had been looking at the wrong people in that photo. Who could have had a grudge against Gerta? And why?

The car Gerta was in passed a little park, then slowed. After a moment, it pulled into a long driveway with big wrought iron gates. Something happened then to cover the camera. My heart went cold. Surely, whoever owned the place hadn't come out to hurt an old lady.

"Look," Priya said, pointing out the window, to where someone was flying a kite near a logo flag waving in the stiff wind. "It's the park they just passed."

The only thing to do was look for the long driveway with the wrought iron gates, hoping we weren't too late. We finally spotted it and drove up to the entry. It was a ranch. Not Southfork but still fancier than anything I'd ever seen in real life, with a mansion and cars lining the giant drive. One of those cars was a long black limo with a *Just Married* decal on the back window. Either someone who lived here was about to get married or someone had rented out this place for their nuptials. No matter which, why would Gerta be brought here?

"Now what?" Aunt Brenda asked.

A guy with a tablet computer came up to the car. Annamaria rolled the manual window down. The guy asked, "Name?"

Annamaria looked flustered. "Annamaria Plunk."

The guy frowned down at his tablet. "I don't have you on the list."

"We wouldn't be," I said quickly. Dang. Why wouldn't we be on his list? I had to think fast. "We're the surprise entertainment the groom ordered for the bride."

All of the Ah-ah-ahs nodded vigorously. The guy looked skeptically at all the old ladies in the car with me.

I sighed. I didn't like to play the fame card, mainly because I hadn't been the biggest success. After the band broke up, my solo career hadn't taken off. But there was only one way to salvage this situation. I rolled my window down too. "I'm Manda Dark. Formerly of Dark Night of the Soul. These lovely ladies are the Ah-ah-ahs. They're some of the most talented comic singers you're ever going to meet."

The guy blinked at me, like maybe he vaguely recognized me. Then he tapped on his tablet—likely Googling me—and looked from it to my face and back again, as if trying to determine if—with a few extra years and none of the makeup (I used to wear a lot of makeup)—I could be the chick on his screen. I guess he decided yes, because he took out a walkie-talkie and waved us through the gate. Someone on the other side was ready to receive us, and they took us straight inside, to where an annoyed wedding planner was muttering loudly about adding us to her schedule.

Aunt Brenda whispered to me, "They aren't actually going to expect us to sing, are they?"

"I hope not," I whispered back. After all, we'd been singing along to the radio on and off this whole road trip. Priya was the only one of the Ah-ah-ahs who could carry a tune.

"This won't do at all," the wedding planner said when she looked up, shaking her head as if in disbelief. "We're talking a hair-and-makeup emergency." She ushered us into a room where several women were busily packing up makeup boxes. When they saw us, they started unpacking. I recognized one of the makeup artists, who only worked with high-profile clients. Whose wedding was this anyway?

While the makeup artists got started on the Ah-ah-ahs, I snuck out to see. I wandered down a few hallways before I finally found the place where the ceremony would be. When I peeked into the room, piled high with flowers and two rows of white chairs, my gaze traveled up the aisle to where a stage had been set up. I gasped. One of my favorite up-and-coming actors was from Dallas—the city, not the show. And there he was, looking all nervous, waiting for his bride. But apparently it was going to be a while before the wedding started, because some of the guests were still milling about. I entered the room, trying not to think about how ironic it was that I was here, crashing a wedding, trying to solve the murder of a party crasher and find my kidnapped friend.

As I checked out the guests, my mouth dropped open. All three of the people who had been in that photo with Gerta and Vinnie were here! It couldn't be a coincidence that Vinnie's murderer took Gerta to this mansion, where these three happened to be attending a wedding. So they shot to the top of my suspects list.

Vinnie's brother was holding a camera, taking shots of the famous people in the room. But he seemed nervous, like he was casing the place. Could he be the one who killed Vinnie? If so, what had he done with Gerta? Please, please let him not have killed her.

Then there was Sapphire Eats, Vinnie's ex, standing near the back, laughing with some guy. She was wearing a deep-blue long-sleeve minidress. (For a wedding? Really?) There was a run in her stockings, and some brown fuzz caught in the sequins on the front of the dress. Could she have gotten in a fight with someone? Maybe Gerta had snapped out of it and managed to escape after the car went through the gates and Sapphire had struggled with her.

The restaurateur whose party Vinnie had crashed was sitting, red in the face, like maybe he'd just been running—or wrestling an old lady into a closet somewhere. Could he have killed Vinnie and then come here as an alibi? And if so, had he walked in with Gerta by his side, docile because she'd been drugged?

Ben waved at the people he was photographing and headed for a side door. At almost the same time, Sapphire seemed to notice the run in her stockings and headed for the back door, presumably to go to the bathroom. Also at the same time, the restaurateur leaned surreptitiously over his phone and started typing what looked like a suspicious text.

Two of my potential suspects were on the move, and I could only follow one of them. But which one?

Sapphire was headed straight for me. The stuff stuck to her dress was actually a small tuft of feathers, maybe from hugging someone else here with an even fancier dress than hers. "Excuse me," she said as she brushed past. Obviously, she didn't recognize me, and her focus on her stockings made me think she wasn't worried about the old woman she'd kidnapped.

I rushed to catch up to Ben, who turned at the doorway when I called his name. I asked him, "Are you the official wedding photographer?"

"Nah," he said. "I'm actually more paparazzi. You know I'm related to Vinnie, from Vinnie Explores, right? Well, I've been thrown out of more celebrity events than my brother."

I winced. If Ben wasn't the killer, he probably didn't know that Vinnie was dead. And I wasn't about to be the one to tell him. "Can I see some of your photos?"

"Sure!" Ben scrolled through his pics, name-dropping all the celebs as he went. He seemed in such good spirits. If he was a murderer, he was also an extremely good actor. And given the number of photos, he'd obviously been here for a while.

He got to one where Sapphire was in the background, coming in the door behind a model who was talking to a B-list actor. I felt my eyes widen, staring at the image. Sapphire had the feathers on her when she got here. And the pattern they've made on the dress—they could well have been from Vinnie's hatband, with its out-of-date rosette of feathers. Maybe she'd thought Vinnie had something hidden in the hat's band and searched it after shooting her ex-boyfriend?

Behind me, the restaurateur let out a gasp—presumably over an answer to his text—and ran out of the room. I could follow him or I could try to find Sapphire.

I went after Sapphire. She wasn't in the ladies' room. But she had been picking the feathers off her dress. She'd left a trail, and I followed it into a parking area behind the mansion, to a garden where things have been set up for the reception.

A car was parked with its trunk open, and not far away, a photo booth with ranch-style photo props stood. Some of the props had been knocked over. Could there have been a struggle? Or was the wind to blame?

Behind the booth, there was a post with two saddled horses tied to it, both placid mares. The post had a large sign on it labeling it a "hitchin' post," with double wedding rings, and arrows indicating that the white horse was for the bride and the brown one for the groom. Nearby stood a waist-high portable watering trough made of garish hot-pink plastic. I was so distracted by the gaudy color that I didn't notice Gerta until she climbed up onto the brown horse from the far side, muttering, "I hate horses."

Tension slid out of my shoulders, the relief melting all the way down to my hands. Gerta must have gotten away from Sapphire and decided to ride to safety. I hurried forward and called her name. As Gerta glanced my way groggily, I said, "Let's go back to the house. It's easier than trying to—"

Just then, Sapphire pulled herself up into the saddle behind Gerta, taking the reins in one hand and pointing a gun at Gerta's back with the other. She spotted me and narrowed her eyes.

"Please," I said as calmly as possible. "Gerta's my friend. Please let her go."

"Not going to happen."

"Don't make things worse," I said. "I get that she saw you shoot your ex-boyfriend."

Sapphire's mouth dropped open, as she probably wondered how I knew.

I continued. "But she's not the only one who knows that." I hesitated, hopefully not long enough for her to realize I was bluffing when I said, "I already texted all the ladies from the RV that you're the killer. I'm sure they've called the police. Let Gerta go, and that's only one murder you'll be charged for, instead of two." I stared at the gun threatening me too, my heartbeat thudding in my ears. "Or three."

"Like I'm going to get caught," Sapphire said. "Killing Vinnie was satisfying, I'll admit. But it's his fault he told me about all the stolen artwork hidden on this old property. It took me a long time to track down Gerta in Florida, and to remind her of how much she wanted to come back to Texas and see Southfork, then make Vinnie think his viewers wanted him to film the place. I went through the trouble of following the RV all the way here, swapping out Gerta's motion sickness pills with something stronger so she wouldn't be in the way when I killed Vin. I'm not stopping now, not when I'm so close to the money. I need the money!" Sapphire's face reddened in rage. "So whatever happens to this old bat isn't my problem."

"Hey!" Gerta protested but fell silent as Sapphire's arm tightened around her, the gun shoved under Gerta's chin.

"Money for what?" I asked Sapphire, playing for time.

"To leave the country. The guy I left Ben for is a stalker, and when I left him for someone else, he just couldn't deal. He put my new boyfriend in the hospital. I'm not going to let him do it to me!"

This was all dramatic enough to have belonged in a soap opera, which felt a bit like reality imitating fiction. I decided not to point out that it would have been easier for her to kill her stalker than to lure Gerta here (for reasons I still didn't get) and kill Vinnie. Either way, she'd still need money to escape the long arm of the law.

"Okay," I told her. "But you have the wrong woman. Gerta's a chef. She can't help you. Lydia's the one who used to be a thief or a spy or something."

Sapphire leveled the gun at me. "Don't treat me like I'm stupid. Vinnie told me his aunt was the one who knew where to find the stolen artwork."

"There is no artwork," Gerta protested weakly, seeming more alert. "I sold it, years ago. The restaurant was in trouble. I needed to keep my family's inheritance safe."

Sapphire's eyes glinted with anger. "Well, let's just go over to the old bunkhouse and see if you're telling the truth." Sapphire gestured at me with the gun. "And as for you. You know too much."

I ducked as the gun went off, then gasped when I realized I was all in one piece, instinctively touching my chest and arms to make certain there really wasn't a bullet hole. Gerta had smacked at Sapphire's hand at the last second, and the shot angled up. Almost giddy with relief, I crawled behind the hot-pink horse trough. My panicked brain randomly thought, *where on earth would you buy something like that?*

The noise brought the security guys from the venue running.

Sapphire let out a frustrated grunt. "Later, you're totally dead."

She kicked the horse, and she and Gerta went galloping away.

"Are you okay?" one of the security guards asked, rushing toward me. "Did she shoot at you?"

I shouted, "She has my friend. I have to stop her," as I untied the white mare from the sickeningly cute "hitchin' post."

I gulped at the very thought of getting back onto a horse. I hadn't ridden since the day I had been literally pulled off my palomino and forced to leave the ranch, after my dad had disappeared and my mom had stopped going to work. That was when we'd moved in with Aunt Brenda. But Sapphire had Gerta on the brown mare and they were already disappearing into the distance.

So I swung up into the white mare's saddle. It was festooned with flowers and lace, ready for the bride to literally ride off into the sunset. I was trembling and the mare caught my nervousness and started dancing sideways. It felt like a lot farther down to the ground than it had when I'd been a teenager.

"Lady, you need to get down from there," the security guy said.

"Sorry!" I shouted, kicking the horse into a gallop and balancing into the momentum. It felt familiar, even after so many years.

I caught up with Gerta and Sapphire almost at the abandoned building, which didn't even look like part of the ranch. Sapphire took another shot at me, but it's really hard to hit a moving target from on horseback. If she could get to the building, she'd have a shielded place to shoot from. And if there really wasn't any art, she would probably shoot Gerta and then try to disappear.

I had to stop them right now. So I urged the mare even faster. When I'd been barrel racing, I'd spent a little time with the trick-riding clowns, and I'd learned a few things, including how to transfer from one mount to another. I'd only done it a couple of times, and I'd been a lot younger and more flexible then. And I hadn't been trying to get onto a horse currently carrying an armed angry woman actively trying to keep me from transferring over, who would have to be knocked off before I could get on. Thankfully, Sapphire seemed to realize she couldn't shoot well over her shoulder and was concentrating on getting away, so she didn't realize when I'd gotten close enough that I might be able to jump on her horse.

Maneuvering the white mare close to the brown one, I reached out and touched the other saddle. Sapphire jerked the gun my way, as Gerta cried, "I think I'm going to be sick."

"Don't you dare." Sapphire aimed the gun back at Gerta.

I slammed Sapphire with my elbow. She lost her balance, and with the help of a nice push from Gerta, she fell off the other side of the brown mare, dropping the gun. She went down cursing my very existence, and kept doing so from the ground, so she probably wasn't badly hurt. Which was good. I didn't want injuring her on my conscience. She stayed down, though, clutching her ankle.

But Gerta was still groggy, and obviously had no idea how to stop a galloping horse with the reins flopping up against its neck. I had to do something before she fell and got hurt. Desperately hoping I still had the upper body strength for this, I grabbed onto the back of the other saddle and wrenched myself over onto the horse behind Gerta. *Yes!* I reached around her for the reigns and slowed the horse. The other mare kept up with us as we cantered over toward the building.

Gerta moaned. "I'm going to be sick."

Then she slumped forward, off balance dead weight. I managed to pull the horse to a halt before losing my grip on Gerta, who jolted back to wakefulness and followed up on her threat, over the horse's side. After that, she seemed clearer, but without saying anything, she pulled her leg over out of the saddle.

"Don't get off. We have to go," I said urgently.

"You go," Gerta said. "I'd rather die than do that again."

That was likely to happen if Sapphire could shake off the pain and hobble our way with the gun. Still, I wasn't just going to leave Gerta there. Maybe we could hide inside the building. Find something to use to defend ourselves, until help arrived. Surely the security guys would arrive soon.

Gerta was already halfway off the mare anyway, so there wasn't much choice. I helped her slide safely to the ground. Then I dropped the reins over the horse's head, hoping the horse would stay ground-tied. There wasn't time to do more than that. I pushed Gerta to walk quickly as we went inside the building. I locked the door behind me. It seemed pretty sturdy. There was only one window. I managed to push a big piece of furniture in front of it before turning to survey the space.

Everything was dusty. This had been a working bunkhouse at one point, and the furniture and odds and ends of discarded clothes and even a few ancient dirty dishes were still there to prove it. Gerta yawned as I followed her toward a door that looked like a closet. Maybe there was something we could use in there.

"Are you okay?" I asked.

"I feel a lot better now that I'm not on that horse. But my head is killing me. And I'm not sure what happened that was real and what wasn't. Vinnie—he'd dead right?"

"I'm sorry," I said.

She winced as she accepted her loss.

I asked, "Was that true what you said? About selling the art?"

"All but this." Gerta opened the closet door and removed a hidden panel. There in the back was a picture of a windmill, maybe eight inches square. She took it out and gazed at it. "Bernard loved this picture. So I left it here, where he had been happy."

"Who was Bernard?" I asked.

"My husband," she said. "He made some mistakes, but he retired from that life and spent time working on this ranch. We met here while I was negotiating prices on beef for my first restaurant. He always meant to come back for the art, but he wound up in jail, for things he had done years before."

It was so tragic and a bit romantic. I looked at the painting of the windmill. It was okay. Not stunning. I doubted it would be the one piece of art I'd keep in her situation. But what did I know? Maybe it was worth millions.

There was a commotion outside. *Oh, no. Had Sapphire gotten here?* I peeked out a crack between the window and the piece of furniture and blew out a deep breath. The security guys must have called the cops. One uniformed officer had Sapphire's gun in an evidence bag, while another was helping her stand, despite her weak ankle. They were not far away from the building. She must have crawled here from where she fell off the horse.

The cops were going to notice the two horses tied up outside. We'd have to explain why Sapphire tried to kill us. We couldn't not tell the truth, even though explaining what happened would include explaining about the murder and the kidnapping and the stolen art, not to mention how we all borrowed—okay stole—a car. I told Gerta, "We have to go out there and talk to them."

"I know." Gerta put the windmill picture back into the closet and replaced the hidden panel. Her secret was safe, once again. "When we're done with the cops, I hope you all will still go with me to Southfork. I still can't believe what happened to Vinnie wasn't a nightmare. He was so young, so alive, and to see him breathe his last—" She shuddered. "He would want me to finish his video. It feels right."

"It does," I said. "For Vinnie, and for the rest of us too. It would be sad to come all this way and never make it to Southfork."

Though the real mystery had been far more intense than watching any soap opera. I hoped seeing the set wouldn't be a letdown—for any of us Ah-ah-ahs.

AMBER ROYER writes the Chocoverse comic telenovela-style foodie-inspired space opera series and the Bean to Bar Mysteries. She also teaches creative writing and is an author coach. Amber and her husband live in the Dallas/Fort Worth area, where you can often find them hiking or taking landscape/architecture/wildlife photographs. If you are very nice to Amber, she might make you cupcakes. Chocolate cupcakes, of course! Amber blogs about creative writing technique and all things chocolate at www.amberroyer.com.

STOOD UP

By Dänna Wilberg

Detective Charles "Chick" Frye sat in one of the red leather booths at Campisi's Egyptian Restaurant, dressed in a new pair of sable calfskin cowboy boots and a baby-blue shirt that matched his eyes. He wiped his palms on his black 511 jeans and deposited four quarters into the tabletop jukebox that sat below a photo of Joe Campisi and Jack Ruby. Chick had loved the history of the place ever since he was a kid, intrigued by stories of Mafia connections and celebrities who were served specially prepared meals in the basement, away from Campisi's regular patrons. In fact, Jack Ruby had visited Campisi's the night before he shot Lee Harvey Oswald on November 24, 1963.

Chick's finger was hovering over the red button connecting him to Dean Martin's "Everybody Loves Somebody" and Bobby Darin's "Mack the Knife" when his phone vibrated across the table. Layla? Maybe she was calling to explain why she was so late. But then he saw the incoming number. Annoyed, he swiped the screen. "Frye."

The voice on the other end sounded apologetic. "Sorry to bother you, Chick—I know this is a big night for y'all—but we got us a dead body."

"Where's Stevens?" Chick usually worked with Jay Peters, but Stevens was supposed to be filling in for Chick tonight—a favor. Some favor.

Chick pictured the Dallas PD's gum-popping dispatcher twirling her hair. Twenty-three with a bachelor's degree in literature—but you couldn't take the teenager out of Stacy Reynolds.

"He had a big break in another case and is out interviewing a witness."

"Well then, I guess you better tell me what'cha got."

"You're gonna *love* this one. A man named Benito Juarez reported a body impaled on one of the bronze longhorn statues at Pioneer Plaza park."

Chick clicked on his mobile notepad and keyed in the man's name, along with "PPP." "What time did the call come in?"

"Eight fifteen." After a silent beat, Stacy sighed. "She didn't show, did she?"

"What gives you that idea?"

"Your tone is practically draggin' on the floor. Can I let Peters know you're available?"

"Sure," he said, glancing at the empty space across the table. "Tell him I'm on my way."

He pressed the red button, tossed a twenty on the table, and listened to Dean croon as he walked out the door. *Maybe next time.*

Fifteen minutes later, Chick pulled in beside a patrol car with flashing lights. He showed his badge to the two officers cordoning the area with yellow crime-scene tape. Chick sidled up to Peters. "Jeezus. That's Lanky Dave."

Peters folded his arms across his middle-age paunch. "Poor bastard. What a way to go."

Lanky Dave's head hung to one side, mouth open, eyes staring into space, as if he were spellbound—or couldn't believe his misfortune. There was little blood around the bronze horn protruding from his chest, indicating the display was an afterthought. "Any gunshot wounds?"

Peters shook his head. "Nope."

"It's still light out." Barely 8:30. "No one saw anything?"

Peters stuffed one freckled hand into his pocket and jingled his change. "Nope. Then again, everyone knows Lanky Dave is a piece of shit—if they did see something, it may not have been worth their time to report it."

"What about the guy who called it in?"

"He's over there." Peters pointed. "He's from Fort Worth— probably doesn't know Lanky Dave's reputation."

Chick slipped on nitrile gloves and examined the body. *No bruising around the neck.* He pushed up one of the victim's sleeves, then the other. Dave's arms looked like he'd been attacked by a woodpecker—or a nail gun. But Chick knew Dave was a user, so the marks were no surprise. What he was looking for were fresh tracks. One mark looked a little tacky. "We'll have to see what shows up in his tox screen. I'll bet you a moon pie he was dead before he was mounted." Chick's eyes followed the herd of larger-than-life-sized bronze longhorns that trailed through the park in a simulated cattle drive. The artist, Robert Summers, devoted his talents to the people of Dallas, supplying them with forty steer, three cowboys on horseback, and one lone horse. Whoever was responsible for Lanky Dave's murder showed no respect for the man's generosity.

Chick leaned in and sniffed the body. "Smell that?"

Peters moved in close for a whiff. "Barbecue?"

Chick grinned. "That's not barbecue. That's the scent of a very expensive old-fashioned."

"You mean one of those smoky numbers they serve at the speakeasy?"

"Yup. There's no mistaking that aroma."

"Smells like barbecue to me." He nudged Chick. "Here come the wedding crashers."

Detectives McCavity and Lawrence sauntered up to the crime scene. McCavity resembled a cross between Liam Neeson and Jackie Chan. Lawrence bested Chick's six-foot-two frame by three inches. The timbre of his deep southern drawl mimicked Barry White.

"Lookee here, it's pretty boy Frye." Lawrence patted Chick on the back.

Chick flicked the man's hand away. "What are you two doing here? Krispy Kreme out of doughnuts?"

McCavity snickered. "We heard the call on the radio—never saw anyone gored before."

Lawrence held his focus on Chick. "Thought you was out with Miss *Lay-la Barnes*."

"She didn't show."

"Man," he said, taking one step back, his white teeth sparkling against his dark skin. "I guess it doesn't matter that you look like Elvis. If a woman ain't interested, she ain't interested."

"Thanks for your support."

"Forget about her, man. She ain't worth that expensive cologne you're wearing or them sexy boots. Plenty of women in Dallas who'd love to date a guy that works twenty-four seven and is never home for Christmas."

"What about Rae-Rae, she complaining?"

"My lady knows that every precious moment spent with me is worth the wait." He gestured to his genitals and flashed Chick a big grin.

"Yeah, yeah, brag on. You'll see. One day Layla will be keeping my bed warm, and when she does…"

Just then, a petite young woman wearing fluorescent-pink jogging shorts and a tight tank top that left nothing to the imagination approached. "Detective Frye?"

Chick cleared his throat and put his eyes back into his head. "Yes, can I help you?"

"I was told you were the one to give this to." She handed Chick a crumpled piece of paper with a pencil drawing of a man impaled on a longhorn.

"Where did you get this?"

"I was jogging on South Griffin, across from McDonald's. I stopped to tie my shoelace. It was practically underfoot."

"And you just happened to pick it up."

"I was intrigued. My brother is a comics illustrator, thought I'd show it to him. And then when I ran down Young Street and saw y'all…"

Peters plucked the paper from Chick's fingers, gave it a quick glance, and deposited it into a plastic baggie. "Fingerprints," he said, nodding to the woman.

"Yeah, Miss—" Chick's eyes gravitated to the woman's left ring finger.

"Angela Newell." She stuck out one dainty hand. "Pleased to make your acquaintance."

Chick pulled off his gloves, gave her hand a gentle squeeze, and said, "You'll have to come down to the station. We need to get your prints. Elimination. You touched the drawing."

"Now? I mean— I'm not—" Angela gestured to her outfit, making all eyes follow her hand from her full bosom to her shapely legs.

Chick remained businesslike. "Do you live far from here?"

"Two blocks that way," she said, pointing west.

"I'll have an officer drive you home so you can change, but first, I'd like to ask you a few questions. I promise not to keep you long." The other men chuckled softly. Chick flashed the men his serious mug. *"Not a word."*

● ● ●

After visiting Dave's mother to break the news—not that she'd seemed to care—they headed to J. Theodore restaurant, in Frisco. Chick acquired that week's password from the hostess, picked up the red phone in the antique phone booth, and waited for the "librarian" to answer. "Edgar Allan Poe," he said into the receiver. Beyond the phone booth, a wall of shelves lined with books slid to the right, revealing the not-so-secret passage to Rare Books Bar—the speakeasy inside the restaurant. Inside,

Lacey Ingram strummed her guitar and sang a Linda Ronstadt tune, her southern twang cutting through the din of voices filling the hazy room.

Chick and Peters waded through the crowd at the bar until they reached the brass rail that separated them from Kelli Green, the bartender.

"You two are partying a little early tonight," she said. "What's the occasion?" Her heavily lined eyes fixed on Chick.

"You been here all night?" he asked.

Kelli smiled. "Got here at four. Why? Am I in trouble or somethin'?"

Chick pulled up an image of Lanky Dave on his phone. "Did you see this man here today?"

"Yeah, around six o'clock. We weren't busy yet. He ordered a smoky old-fashioned. Said he was waitin' on someone."

"Did that someone show up?"

"Not that I recall. He barely finished his drink. Got a phone call and left."

"Damn." Chick slid his phone back into his pocket.

Kelli kept working, plunking a clean glass filled with ice on the bar, pouring a shot of Jack Daniels, followed by a splash of water. "If it's any consolation," she said, "I heard him mention Gatsby's 'fore he left."

Chick blew Kelli a kiss. "Love ya, babe. Thanks."

Kelli caught the kiss in her right hand. "Uh, huh." As Chick turned away, Kelli said loud enough for everyone to hear, "One of these days, I'm gonna ride that cowboy."

● ● ●

Peters pulled up to the curb in front of the Gatsby Nightclub. Chick eyed the place through the smudged passenger window. "Don't you ever wash your car?"

"Yeah, when I get a day off. You wanna drive next time?"

"Maybe." He exited slowly, taking in every inch of the club's art-deco exterior. Four scantily clad marble statues in recessed alcoves flanked the entryway, two on each side. Black half-dome awnings covered two large wooden doors with signature brass door handles shaped like the letter G. Above, on the second floor, a balustrade railing lined a covered patio, and above that, glass panels revealed a rooftop deck. Gatsby's lived up to the character's reputation, boasting of decadence and overindulgence. *Life's one big party.*

The two men pushed through one elaborate door. It was late. The place was nearly empty.

"Help you?"

Chick pivoted toward a sultry voice. The woman entering the room in a gold flapper dress oozed sex appeal.

Chick held his phone with Lanky Dave's photo inches from her pretty face. "Seen this guy today?"

"Who wants to know?" She glared at him with sapphire eyes that belonged in a jeweler's case. Chick produced his badge. "He was found murdered tonight. I have it on good authority he stopped here on his way to the morgue."

"He was here," she said, breaking eye contact. "Close to seven. Happy hour was in full swing. The place was packed."

Chick noticed a small serpent tattoo beneath her right earlobe. "Did you speak to him?"

"No. He didn't stay long. Left with some guy I've never seen before."

"What did the guy look like?"

"I don't know—he was big. Average-looking," she said, her tone blasé. "Nothing memorable."

Peters stepped forward, a fake smile plastered on his face. "Is that the best you can do?"

She tilted her head, and raised one pierced brow. "He looked like he could kick *your* ass."

Chick handed her his card. "Perhaps your surveillance tapes will help us identify this Mr. Big."

"Perhaps they will. But I believe you'll need a warrant." She paused, letting her words linger. "Now, if you'll excuse me, I have work to do."

She didn't wait for approval. She sauntered out of the room the same way she had come in, leaving the two men stuck in the moment.

* * *

"What do we know?" Chick asked as they sat in Peters's vehicle, sipping coffee and nibbling on McDonald's French fries.

Peters licked salt from his fingers. "He was at J. Theodore's around six, Gatsby's shortly after. Takes at least twenty-five minutes to get from point A to point B. Leaves with a big average-looking guy. Ends up impaled before nine. Busy guy." Peters popped another French fry into his mouth. "Probably pissed off one of his suppliers."

"That drawing…his death was premeditated. Did he owe someone money? Come up short on his stash? Woman scorned?"

"You heard what Dave's own mother said. He was scum. Could've been all of the above."

Chick nodded. "Yeah, I agree, but something doesn't feel right. We're missing a piece of the puzzle."

* * *

The next morning, the medical examiner confirmed Chick's suspicion. Lanky Dave had died from an overdose. He'd had enough opioids in his system to kill two people, maybe three.

He hadn't heard from Layla since she stood him up last night. Any other girl would've at least sent him a text, called, left a message. *Something.* Not Layla. And he knew better than to push his luck. "I have a career," she had told him. "I don't have time to put a Band-Aid on every hurt feelin' or bruised ego." Why he tortured himself by thinking she would give up an acting career, or anything, to become his main squeeze was ridiculous. *I'd be better off with a dog.*

He thought about Angela Newell. *Now there's a sweet one.* She was *so* willing to help. He'd taken in every nuance while they were talking. She'd seemed to like him too. It was the way she'd stolen glances at him as he wrote down her answers. The way her lips had softened when she formed her words. The way she'd leaned forward to give him a better view of her bosom. He found her discovery rather coincidental, but this was Dallas. Weird stuff happened in Dallas all the time. But still, something was holding him back.

Ethics? Unlikely. After all, it wouldn't be unethical to pursue her once the case was over. The problem, he knew deep down, was that Lawrence was right. He was married to his job. Not many women bought into a cop's lifestyle, especially a cop who struggled with coincidences.

Peters called. "We got another stiff."

"Where?"

"Fountain Place. The person who called it in thought the victim was one of our city's urban outdoorsmen, drowned in one of the fountains."

"And?"

"The guy has no ID, but he's dressed too nice to be homeless."

"Who called it in?"

"A janitor spotted him from a fifth-floor window. I sent a couple of guys to get his statement."

"I'll be right there."

● ● ●

By the time Chick arrived at the downtown skyscraper, the fountains in its surrounding plaza were cordoned off with yellow tape, and the medical examiner was examining the waterlogged body on the lawn. It was the same pathologist who'd dealt with Lanky Dave's gored body. Chick bent down next to him.

"No visible wounds," the ME said.

Chick glanced up at Peters. "Did we get the warrant for the surveillance tapes at Gatsby's?"

"Not yet. You thinkin' what I'm thinkin'?"

Chick rose and brushed the creases from his black trousers. "This guy looks pretty big to me. You?"

"Yeah. He looks like he could've lifted Lanky Dave with one hand tied behind his back.

Let me give Lawrence a call, see if he can light a fire under the judge."

Chick perused the grounds. It was unlikely he'd find a witness. A lot of homeless people relied on the fountains to beat the heat when the temps climbed; however, when the weather turned cool, they scattered throughout the city.

As the paramedics put the body on a gurney, Chick caught the ME's attention. "Think he drowned? Or could it be a drug overdose, like the other guy?"

"'Could be' an overdose," he said, using air quotes. "His lips are blue-tinged. Cyanosis indicates lack of oxygen before he hit the water, but I can't be one hundred percent sure of anything until I run some tests and check out *all* of my findings."

"When will you know?"

"I'll do a tox screen when I get back to the lab."

"Any idea what time he died? What about prints?"

"From the maceration to his skin, I'd say he's been in the water at least five, six hours—so don't expect fingerprints right away." He removed his nitrile gloves with a snap. "I'll do what I can and get back to you ASAP."

Chick met up with Peters by his car. "What did Lawrence say?"

"He said to come by after five to pick up the warrant." He chuckled. "Lawrence must have a magic wand."

"Yeah—a magic wand that keeps the judge's daughter *very* happy."

Over at the Corner Bakery Cafe, Peters ordered an Uptown Turkey Avocado club, and Chick ordered chicken carbonara pasta. They sat in silence watching people mill back and forth by the railroad tracks. Chick's eyes grew large when the waitress set his partner's sandwich down in front of him. "How you gonna fit that thing in your mouth?"

Peters picked up the triple-decker sandwich in his large mitts. "Watch me." Chick twirled pasta into a spoon with his fork, swiped off the loose ends, and popped the fork into his mouth. Lost in thought, Chick practically inhaled his meal without a word.

Peters broke their silence. "Heard from Layla?"

"Nah. She's busy. Probably got another gig or somethin'."

"Did you call her? Maybe she's waiting for you to make a move."

"She stood me up. She can call me."

"Yeah, but maybe she thinks you're mad at her."

"I should be. She could've texted me—"

"You're right. It's rude to leave someone hangin' like that."

"Maybe it's a blessing she didn't show. Couldn't very well bring a date to a murder scene."

"Kelli Green has the hots for you—"

"Kelli Green has the hots for everybody."

"What happened with the chick with the drawing?"

"Angela Newell?"

"Angela is it?"

"Pretty girl. She kinda liked me, I think."

"Ask her out."

"She probably has a boyfriend. A girl that good lookin'--"

"See? That's what's wrong with you! *You're* good lookin', but you're dumb when it comes to chicks, *Chick*." Peters picked up his pickle spear and waved it to get his point across. "Women want to be pursued. Chase 'em a little. They like to play hard to get. You chase a little more, and before you know it—they let you catch 'em."

"Is that how you ended up with Colleen?"

"Damn straight!"

"I'll keep that in mind. Meanwhile, we have two stiffs and no leads."

After lunch, he and Peters hit the streets, collecting what information they could from Dave's clientele, gleaning only one thing, the guy was despised by all. Then they picked up and executed the warrant at Gatsby's and returned to the station, where they pored over the footage. There was more to review, but they stopped when they saw Lanky Dave meet up with the man found floating in the fountain.

Usually Chick would be excited about connecting two cases. But tonight he felt drained, and Peters must have noticed.

"Go home," Peters said. "Colleen is at the movies tonight with her mom. I can stay and finish up the tapes." Chick didn't debate.

It was after nine when he got home. He opened his fridge, stared a few minutes, grabbed a carton of milk, and shut the door. He pulled a box of cereal from one cupboard, a bowl from another. He glanced at the time. Too late to call? *What the hell.*

"Layla? Hey, it's Chick."

"Chick, oh my God, how are you?" Her voice sounded breathy; her tone sounded busy.

"Good. Missed you the other night."

"The other night?" He imagined her perfect brows cinching together.

"Yes. We had a date. We were supposed to meet at Campisi's."

"Oh, Chick, I'm so sorry. I completely forgot. I—"

"It's okay. We can try another time. How have you been?"

"Things have been hectic. In fact, I really can't talk right now. I'm at the hospital—my sister."

"Wow, sorry to hear—she's gonna be okay, right? I mean—"

"I gotta go, Chick. Talk soon. Bye."

Chick stared at the phone. He hadn't known Layla had a sister. Could be the stress, but Layla hadn't seemed herself on the call. *She completely forgot.*

He swiped his screen to text: *Which hospital? I'd like to send flowers.*

Her text came almost immediately: *Please don't.*

Chick tossed his phone on the counter. It rang midair.

"Buddy!" It was Peters.

"What's up? My cornflakes are getting soggy."

"Thought you'd like to know who else I saw on the surveillance tape."

"I give up—who?"

"Layla Barnes."

"Layla? You've got to be kidding me!" His fingers plowed through his thick black hair. "There must be some mistake. I just spoke with her. She's at the hospital—her sister's sick."

Peters bristled. "Why would I say it was her if it wasn't?"

"I just don't understand, that's all. Why wouldn't she—"

"It almost seemed like she was stalking Lanky Dave and the other guy. You gotta see for yourself."

Chick's appetite went down the drain along with the cereal he poured in the sink. *No wonder she didn't show.*

● ● ●

Peters sat alone in his dimly lit cubicle. Chick came up behind him. "You sure know how to cheer a guy up."

"That's right—you're *sad*. Mea culpa."

"Let me see what you found." Chick pulled a chair next to Peters and straddled it, facing the screen. Peters pressed play. Chick watched his crush slither through a crowd of drunks at

Gatsby's, trying to conceal herself behind the tall and wide. Her sights were set on the two men at the bar. Lanky Dave and the mystery man found floating in the fountain. When the two men got up to leave, Layla disappeared into the crowd. "Where'd she go?" Chick leaned closer to the monitor.

"Be patient." Peters tipped back in his chair. "There." He froze the image of Layla exiting through a side door.

Chick scoffed, "Doesn't prove anything."

"No, but it sure as hell puts her near our first vic close to his time of death."

"Wish we knew who the second vic is. The ME hasn't gotten back to me yet with his prints. Have the prints come back on the drawing?"

Peters shuffled through a stack of papers on his desk. "Have you checked your email?"

Chick did a one-handed scroll on his phone. "Got it." He read silently, and then, "Holy shit."

Peters peered over his shoulder and read out loud. "Four sets of prints: one unidentified man, Lanky Dave, Angela Newell, and Lindsey Barnes. Layla's sister?"

Chick tossed his phone on Peters's desk. "What the hell is going on?"

"Only one way to find out. You driving? Or am I?"

"I'll drive. My jeep is clean."

After calling three popular hospitals in the area, Chick found a Lindsey Barnes registered at Medical City Hospital in North Dallas. The two men showed their badges at the front desk and were escorted to the ICU. Chick saw Layla standing over a young woman with blond hair, like hers. As if she sensed his stare, she turned, shock written all over her face. She burst through the door, madder than a hornet.

"You couldn't leave it alone, could you? Had to stick your nose where it doesn't belong!"

"Come, sit down." Chick took her arm and led her to a private area to talk. "How do you know Lanky Dave?"

Her face paled ghostly white. Tears filled her eyes. "He gave my sister the drugs that almost killed her. I don't know if she'll ever be the same. Her brain, it's—" She buried her face in her hands and sobbed. If she was acting, she deserved an Academy Award.

"Was your sister using?"

"It was a phase, nothing more!"

"And you're positive she got her drugs from Lanky Dave."

"Yes."

Peters presented a photo of the mystery man. "What about this guy? You know him?"

Layla looked up, her green eyes swimming in tears. "His name is Ivan. That's all I know."

"Ivan is dead."

Chick paid close attention to Layla's reaction. He wanted to believe she had no connection to Lanky Dave's death or Ivan's, but it was too coincidental that both men were murdered soon after Layla spied on them at the bar. "Did you have Dave killed?"

"Why would you even ask me that?"

Chick matched her flippant response with an ironclad answer. "We saw you on the surveillance tape at Gatsby's."

• • •

Lawrence's eyes grew as big as saucers when he saw Layla enter the squad room, followed by Chick and Peters. "Man, is that the only way Chick's gonna get a date with that girl?" he said to McCavity, who chortled a response.

Chick sent them a death stare before retrieving the sketch Angela Newell had found near the park from the evidence room.

"A jogger found this," Chick said, handing it to Layla in a protective baggie. "Your sister's prints are on it."

"I have no idea why—my sister can't draw a stick figure."

"Somethin's gotta give, Layla," Chick said, his voice gentle. "Two men were found dead within hours of each other. We have your sister's prints on the drawing, and we have you at Gatsby's right before Dave was impaled at Pioneer Park. Now I know you don't have the muscle to physically make that happen, but Ivan looks like he could do the job."

Layla moaned, as if her soul was trying to escape her body. The haunted look in her eyes gave Chick goose bumps. Yet his heart broke seeing her so vulnerable.

Her story began like the narration one would hear at the beginning of a movie…clear, dramatic, intense. She spoke of the closeness she and her sister shared, how as young girls they had vowed to take care of each other after their parents divorced and pursued new interests. "Lindsey never found her way…" She explained her sister's battle with drugs, rehab, her failure to get it right. "At first it was just pills, then it was pills and booze. I worried about her all the time. But when I found out she was using heroin, I lost it—I knew something needed to be done." She closed her eyes. "I went to see Dave." Her eyes flashed open. "He blew me off."

"What did you do?"

"I offered him ten-thousand dollars to stay away from my sister. He changed his tune."

"What were you doing at Gatsby's the night he was killed?"

"I was supposed to deliver the cash to Dave at the speakeasy in J. Theodore. I got stuck downtown, so he suggested we meet at Gatsby's. When I got there, he was with Ivan."

Peters piped in, "Who is Ivan?"

"Dave's supplier."

Chick nodded. "Then what happened?"

"They left, so I followed them to the park. No one else was there—I hid behind an oak tree. Dave and Ivan were arguing. Ivan said something about what he was going to do to him. Then he shoved a piece of paper in Dave's face, smirking as Dave's eyes widened, like he got off on Dave looking scared. Then I saw him jab Dave with something. After a few seconds, Dave collapsed." Layla began to tremble. "Ivan carried Dave over to the longhorn, lifted him up, and pushed his body so hard—"

Chick patted her hand. "You're doing fine. Go on."

"I wanted to scream, but then I saw…" Layla's words hung in the air.

Chick turned to Peters. "Get her some water." Peters grabbed a bottle from his bottom drawer and handed it to Chick.

Layla took a sip, her gaze seemingly fixed on a memory she couldn't shake. Chick nudged her forward. "What did you see Layla?"

She glared at him. "Isn't that enough?"

"Is it?" he snapped back. Their battle ended when he resumed his gentle tone. "What did you see?"

"My sister," she said, dropping her head in defeat. "I could tell by the tone of her voice she was angry."

"Could you hear what she was saying?"

"No. He kept pointing to what I assumed was the same piece of paper he'd shown Dave. My sister snatched it out of his hand and shoved it in her pocket."

"Then what happened?"

"Lindsey headed toward South Griffin."

"She must've dropped the drawing," Peters said.

"What did *you* do?"

"I waited until Ivan left—I was too terrified to move." She exhaled. "Once he was gone, I went after my sister."

"Was that the last time you saw him?"

Layla's red-rimmed eyes seemed to plead with him. "Yes." She took another sip of water and straightened her posture. "As I said, my aim was to find Lindsay. She wasn't in her usual haunts. I was afraid of what she would do, having seen Dave's body like that. I was desperate to find her." Layla looked away, as if the memory was too painful.

"What time did you find your sister? And where?"

Fresh tears formed in Layla's eyes. "I found her wandering by Fountain Plaza. She still had elastic tubing wrapped around her arm, so I knew she'd just shot up. She was slurring, her lips turning blue. We checked into the ER around two-thirty. They gave her Narcan." Her bottom lip quivered. "We were lucky."

Peters glanced at Chick. "So, you don't know if Ivan was still alive? That's where he was found—Fountain Plaza."

"No."

Chick intervened. "And you didn't see your sister push Ivan into the fountain?"

"No. If Ivan was there, I didn't see him. Maybe somebody else did it."

Months later, Chick deposited four quarters into the jukebox at Campisi's and waited for Dean's voice to validate the ache in his heart. Everybody loves somebody, true. But sometimes a heart gets misdirected. *Until something happens and love finds its way.*

Layla's misdemeanor for not reporting Lanky Dave's murder had resulted in a fine and a month's probation. He'd thought she'd call after her sentencing hearing, but she didn't, and he'd eventually decided to move on. After all, it's not like they ever were a thing. When he'd later heard she'd moved to LA without so much as a goodbye, he'd been surprised to realize it didn't bother him. Not much anyway.

As to Lindsey, he'd found out from a friend in the DA's office that she'd gone to rehab. She was never indicted for Ivan's death.

"Is someone joining you this evening, Mr. Frye?"

Chick checked his watch and glanced at the door. "Yes," he replied, his mind swinging from listening to Dean's slouchy baritone voice to the situation at hand. If only his thoughts could manifest a glimpse into his future.

The door opened, and Angela stepped in, searching. When she spotted Chick, her smile lit up the room.

Chick stood, gave her a warm smile back, and settled next to her in the booth.

"I'm so glad you called," she said.

"I'm so glad you came," he said. He studied her face for a moment, savoring her beauty.

"I used to come here a lot as a kid," she said. "I love the food—the history. Did you know this was the last place Jack Ruby ate before he shot Oswald?"

Chick's smile faded as he slid a drawing toward her. "I did." He pointed at the photocopy of the sketch she'd given him the night Lanky Dave died. "You're quite the artist. Semi-finalist in the Congressional Art Competition 2009, finalist in The Chelsea International Fine Art Competition 2011. Need I go on?"

The gleam in her eyes hardened. Dean finished his song, and Bobby Darin picked up on cue, crooning about sharks with sharp teeth.

"The night of Lanky Dave's murder," he said, "you told me you found the drawing on South Griffin, that you intended to show it to your brother. Maybe it was the way you held the drawing, like you were comfortable with the subject matter. To me, it seemed too coincidental, so I did some digging and discovered your brother was killed in a motorcycle accident in 2010." Angela's face paled, her words came out flustered. "Did you invite me to dinner to—to interrogate me?"

"How long have you and Lindsey Barnes been lovers?"

Her eyes flashed. "Isn't this entrapment or something?"

"Nope. I'm not asking you to commit a crime. I'm asking for the truth."

"I don't know what you're talking about," she said, brushing away his words with a flick of her wrist. "Would I be here if I was—"

"I know why you're here—for the same reason you showed up at the crime scene. You think you can outsmart us." Chick leaned closer. "We checked surveillance videos from the area where you claimed to have found the drawing, and guess what we saw?" He watched her expression transform, fortify. Suddenly, she wasn't so pretty.

"Lindsey was killing herself. Dave was helping her." Mentioning Dave seem to amalgamate her anger with frustration. "Have you ever loved somebody so much you would do anything to keep them safe?"

"Drug dealers don't bump off their minions without good reason."

Angela sneered. "Ivan didn't need much convincing once word got out that Dave was stealing from him."

"Why kill Ivan?"

She looked away. "Sometimes it's not enough to take care of the infection—you have to eradicate the disease."

Chick gently turned her face toward his. "What happened?"

"I'd been searching for Lindsey for hours. I found her with Ivan at the fountains around two a.m. They were both high."

"Why did you think they were high?"

"I saw two needles lying on the ground. Lindsey was adjusting her clothes, and I saw Ivan zipping his pants. He tucked another packet inside her bra."

"Did you confront them?"

"Lindsey ran off when she saw me. It didn't take a rocket scientist to figure out what was going on, or what Lindsey would do, so I texted Layla, told her where to find her sister."

Chick nodded. "Then what?"

"I told Ivan I wanted to fill him in on what I told the cops about 'finding' the drawing." Angela twisted a red napkin in her hands. "Then, yes, I confronted him about Lindsey."

"What did he say?"

"He asked why I was wasting my time on a junkie whore."

"What did you say?"

"I couldn't speak." Angela stared ahead, as if conjuring the scene. "He turned his back to me. I picked up a rock." She released the napkin. "He never saw it comin'."

"You must've really clobbered him."

"Lucky shot. He didn't even bleed."

"Help me understand—how did he end up in the fountain?"

"He picked himself up and staggered toward the fountain, cussin' and callin' me dirty names."

"And what did you do?"

She tilted her head, her smile wicked. "I pushed him in."

Reaching behind him, Chick tapped the top of the booth. Peters rose and came around to join them, a set of cuffs dangling from one finger.

Chick slid out of the booth and took Angela's hand. "Angela Newell, I am placing you under arrest for the murder of David Dirk and Ivan Minsky. You have the right to remain silent…" While he finished reading Angela her rights, Peters discreetly cuffed her. Then he walked her outside.

Chick assessed the room. The few remaining couples didn't seem fazed by Angela's arrest. They continued to eat, gazing into each other's eyes as if their love shielded them from the ugliness in the world. *If only.*

He threw cash on the table, and headed for the door. *One day I'll find the right girl.* Frank Sinatra agreed, crooning from a nearby jukebox, and Chick smiled. Yep, he might have nothing now, but one day, he'd have it all.

"The best secrets are the most twisted." Sara Shepard's quote from *Twisted* best describes **DÄNNA WILBERG'S** quest to unravel life's mysteries with every keystroke, on every page. Her novels *The Red Chair*, *The Grey Door*, and *The Black Dress*, featuring psychotherapist Grace Simms, pose the question: what do we really know about a person? Dänna's paranormal Borrowed Time series, about a woman who acquires a psychic gift after a near-death experience, is filled with gems from Dänna's experience producing and hosting the TV show *Paranormal Connection* for over fifteen years. Her background as an award-winning scriptwriter and filmmaker further add to the magic of her storytelling. dannawilberg.com

STEER CLEAR

By Mark Thielman

Detective Alpert knew that he should not have slept with his lieutenant's wife.

To be fair, Brittney was the lieutenant's ex-wife, a distinction that seemed more important to Alpert than it did to his commanding officer.

Over his years as a cop, Alpert had benefited from the instructions of many fine partners—patrol officers and detectives. He'd learned to trust their advice. It had become a personal mantra to listen when his partner started talking. However, at Sergeant Reich's retirement party, last night at the Albatross, he should have ignored those whispers emerging from his glass of Jim Beam. Jim had made sure that he noticed Brittney's leather pants. Alpert had always had a fondness for leather. When she shimmied past his barstool, Jim had kindly offered up the opinion that since Brittney and Lieutenant Washington were legally divorced, there would be no problem with a little harmless dancing. After all, the Albatross played Bob Wills and Alpert knew it was a violation of a city ordinance not to dance western swing. Finally, old Jim had suggested that if they left separately, no one would connect the two of them.

The whispers and snickers around the Major Case Division told Detective Alpert that he needed to limit his rule about trusting partners to humans and dogs.

Comey, his latest human partner, hung up the phone. "Lieutenant wants to see you." Comey exhaled, fluttering his walrus-like mustache. "I hope your love life didn't ruin my day."

Alpert rested his elbows on the stack of books he intended to read and massaged his temples. "Is it too late to call in sick?"

Comey's desk abutted Alpert's. He leaned forward, closing the distance between them. "You do remember we're in the personal-responsibility business?"

Alpert stood. "Where was your helpful reminder last night?"

* * *

"A steer-napping?" Alpert asked.

The lieutenant's eyes stayed on his computer. He cocked his head toward the thin file on his desk. "Bluebonnet is a major economic engine for Fort Worth's north side. I've just gotten off the phone with the chief, who had just gotten off the phone with the mayor. They want Blue found quickly."

"But this is the Major Case Division."

The lieutenant turned and faced him. The quivering muscles at the back of his jaws hinted at his rage. "And what exactly does *major case* mean, Detective? When a car gets stolen, the Auto Theft Division gets involved. When a murder occurs, Homicide responds. Last I checked, Fort Worth doesn't have a Cattle Rustling Division. So when the chief says it's a major case, the Major Case Division answers. And I'm sending you."

Alpert glanced at the thin file. "Doesn't look like much to go on."

"The crime just happened. You're a detective. Detect something."

* * *

They crossed the Paddock Viaduct heading north. Comey drove, chewing a hamburger.

Alpert tried not to watch him eat. The greasy smell played enough havoc with his stomach. Instead, he squinted out the window, his eyes facing east, away from the setting sun. He looked at the slow-moving bend of the Trinity River. Water, he thought, from now on I'm drinking nothing but water.

They rolled past car lots and scrapyards. He looked at faded buildings and rusted metal. The scenery matched Alpert's mood. Across Northside Drive, the buildings began to change. The owners worked harder at maintaining the storefronts. They kept the junk hidden out of sight. Here, Fort Worth sought to cash in on its heritage. The city had paved North Main Street with bricks as a throwback to Fort Worth's cattle-driving days along the Chisholm Trail. On both sides of the street, shops sold high-end western wear or tourist tchotchkes. Alpert clutched his head, ignoring them all. The staccato rattling of the Caprice's suspension jabbed at the remnants of his Jim Beam hangover.

A pickup clattered past pulling a horse trailer, amplifying the noise.

Alpert groaned.

"You say anything else?" Comey asked.

"I told him I didn't know the first thing about cows."

"What'd he say?"

"He gave me a look that told me he wouldn't mind too much if I failed. 'You're a Cowtown detective. This is where the West begins. Learn.'"

Comey grunted. "Guess he thought you knew a little something about leather."

They parked alongside a patrol car outside the cattle barn. According to the report, this was the crime scene. A uniformed officer stood talking to a woman in faded jeans, a pearl-snap plaid western shirt, and a weathered cowboy hat. The patrolman broke away and approached the two detectives.

He gestured to the woman. "That's Sarah Ruth. She's the lead drover for Fort Worth's herd."

"Herd?" Alpert asked.

The patrolman nodded. "It's a North Side thing. Every morning, Sarah and her fellow drovers drive the herd down Main Street to a pasture. Every afternoon they bring them back to the barn. Tourists line up to watch."

"Sydney has an opera house. We've got a cattle herd," Comey said.

The patrolman shrugged. He led them over and introduced them to Sarah.

"He tells me that you're the trail boss," Alpert said.

"I am for now." Sarah's lower lip quivered. "Who knows what will happen after this mess?"

Alpert caught a faint whiff of alcohol. He couldn't tell if she was angry or close to tears. "Tell me what happened."

"Me and the other drovers pushed the herd back to the barn like we do every afternoon," Sarah said. "We've got fifteen head we move back and forth. Used to have twenty, but, you know, budget cuts. Each one has its own stall. We got them settled in and then we headed down to the drover's room. That's our office. We got showers and lockers down there. I sent Billy down to check on the livestock. That's when he found Blue missing."

"And where's Billy?" Alpert asked.

"With the others down in the drover's room. Want to go down there?"

Alpert shook his head. "I want to see the stalls first."

Sarah led them into the brick building. Inside it smelled of dust and hay. A large open space was divided into rows of stalls. A wide central path ran down the center. Sarah stopped in front of the first stall.

Comey pointed at a wooden plaque on the pen's gate. It read "Bluebonnet." "Being a detective and all, I'm guessing that this is where you kept him."

Sarah nodded. "First pen inside the door. Blue is the one everyone wants to see."

Alpert studied the barn. He took a few pictures with his phone. The crime-scene guys would shoot more when they arrived, but he liked having a few photographs to accompany his field notes. The pens all looked about the same. They had water lines and troughs. The front of the building held cattle. Horses were stabled in the back. Most of the large animals quietly chewed their food and ignored the detectives. Alpert noticed a plastic bucket fastened to the adjoining pen. Lead ropes hung by the front door. Above a pen on the other side, PVC pipe stretched across the rafters. Alpert noted all these things. What he didn't see were security cameras.

"No video monitoring?" he asked.

Sarah shook her head. "Not in here. We've got cameras outside. They cover the exits."

"Nothing inside at all?"

She shook her head again. "We've asked to put cameras in here. Livestream the herd, but there's only so much money in a city budget. The outside cameras also guard against graffiti taggers."

Alpert felt his phone buzz. He checked the screen. Brittney was calling. He let the phone go to voicemail. She'd been married to a cop. Brittney knew the case came first.

"We'll need to get the video," Comey said.

Sarah nodded. "We pulled it up as soon as we discovered him missing. Nothing to see."

"Can't identify anyone?" Comey asked.

Sarah shook her head. "I mean the cameras don't show Blue leaving."

"Is there another way out?" Alpert asked.

Again, Sarah shook her head. "Just the front and back entrance. Both monitored. The video shows us bringing the herd inside. No cattle left."

"Technical glitch?"

"Tim, one of the drovers, he's a bit of a techie. He says the video looks intact."

Alpert walked down the central aisle. Some of the cattle lifted their heads and gave him a round-eyed passing glance. Others kept their heads down in the troughs outside the gates. "And nobody came in or out?"

"We all came in and out," Sarah said. "But no cattle left the barn."

"You're sure?"

She looked at him and cocked her head. "Look at them. Blue is the biggest of the lot. He weighs about as much as a Toyota. We'd have noticed him leaving the building."

Alpert gazed upward at a row of small windows high on a wall.

"Not without wings," Sarah said in answer to the unasked question.

"Why would someone steal Blue?" Alpert asked instead.

Sarah shrugged. "Why would you steal a Picasso or a Rembrandt?"

Alpert looked at her. He beckoned with his hand for her to elaborate.

"He's a unique, one-of-a-kind animal. Blue is a celebrity. Every year before the Super Bowl we lay out a grid in the pasture. He predicts the winner."

"How does he do that?" Comey asked.

"He drops a cow patty on a square. He has thousands of followers on his Instagram page."

Alpert wished he'd never seen Brittney's leather pants.

"And," Sarah said, "his portfolio outperforms the S&P."

Alpert ventured a guess. "Picked the same way?"

Sarah nodded. "We change the grid, but it's the same cow patty method. The press people call it his Moo-tual Fund."

"Clever," Alpert said.

"The point is, he's a celebrity. A rustler can't just take Blue to a livestock auction and sell him off. He'd be recognized."

Alpert walked over to the nearest pen. The plaque said that this animal was "Lightfoot." He gestured with his hands around Lightfoot's head. "Could someone change his markings with hair dye or shoe polish? It wouldn't wash off until after the sale."

"We've got his DNA on file. We've already sent it off to every auction barn in Texas and Oklahoma."

"Private breeder?" Alpert asked. "Cheaper than buying a prize winner."

"Blue's a steer, not a bull," Sarah said.

Alpert narrowed his eyes.

"Snip." As Sarah spoke, she lowered her hand to her waist and made a scissor motion.

Feeling his face redden, Detective Alpert walked inside Blue's pen. He kept his back to his audience, running his hands along the steel rails of the enclosure as well as the brick back wall. He turned to Comey. "No trap doors."

Comey grunted, making his mustache hairs dance. "Not a parlor trick."

Alpert looked to Sarah. "I think we need to talk to the others."

She led them out of the cattle barn, pausing in front of a display of framed abstract paintings. "I forgot to tell you that Blue is also an artist."

Alpert looked at the paintings, thick brushstrokes slashed across the canvases.

"We fasten a brush to Blue's tail and hold the canvas. He does the rest."

Alpert looked at the paintings again. "Let me guess his favorite color."

Sarah led them on the short walk to the drover's room. As they arrived, an unmarked police car parked. The lieutenant got out, straightened his jacket, and walked in their direction.

"Update me," he said without waiting for an introduction.

"Still early," Alpert said. "Doing the preliminary investigation."

"Mayor's office called. Can we say we're narrowing down the list of suspects?"

Comey shrugged. "We can say a one-ton steer disappeared without a trace."

The lieutenant frowned.

"But we're hopeful that the disappearing steer will magically come back soon."

The lieutenant slowly shook his head and focused on Alpert. "I'd hate to be the detective who had to use the word 'magically' when reporting to the mayor."

Alpert's pocket vibrated. He pulled out his phone and glanced down. "Sorry, got to take this," he said to the lieutenant. Turning away, he spoke loudly enough for all to hear. "Hey, Brittney. Listen, I'm going to have to call you back. I'm in a meeting right now." Alpert held the phone to his ear. He smiled as he turned. His voice sweetened. "I'd like that. Talk soon. Bye, babe."

He watched the lieutenant climb into his car, then slam the door. In seconds, Washington's car sped away.

Comey looked at Alpert. "That lady must have ESP and know the absolute worst time to call."

Alpert shook his head. "Robocall, letting me know my car warranty was about to expire."

● ● ●

The drover's office was a large room furnished with a pair of desks and a table. On the walls hung framed photographs of the herd. Some showed the herd lumbering along on the daily cattle drive. Others showed close-ups of fans, mostly children, rubbing the noses of the cattle. Blue, his broad horns displayed prominently, featured in many of the photographs. Alpert saw men's and women's locker rooms at the back of the room. Around the table, three people sat. Open beer cans rested in front of each of them. A glance at the empty plastic yokes on the table and the half-full trash can told him that nobody was on their first.

When his gaze returned to the table, Sarah was watching him. "Tim here is our resident practical joker. One of his pranks misfired a bit last week. He brought beer to atone." She gestured toward a lanky young man who had a bad attempt at a goatee hanging from his chin.

"This happen often?" Alpert asked.

"Nah," the goatee said, "my jokes usually land."

"I meant the drinking?"

"We're off duty," Sarah said. "Pushing cows is dusty. We sometimes have a beer. Not every day, but you know…"

Alpert nodded. He did know.

They interviewed each drover separately. Destiny reported going down to the barn. Her horse had acted a little sore-footed on the ride back from the pasture. She checked on him. Blue and the rest of the cattle were in their pens. Nothing seemed out of the ordinary. She came back to the office. Tim brought in the beer. She settled in with one, maybe two. Destiny remembered Billy leaving. A few minutes later, he burst into the office, wide-eyed, and reported Blue missing. They all raced down to the pen. Somebody said they needed to check the security tape—Destiny now pointed to the desk holding the monitor—then Sarah and Destiny had raced back while the boys scoured the area looking for the missing steer.

"How did you get a job as a drover?" Alpert asked.

"Did you know that in the 1800s, about a quarter of the cowboys were Black?" Destiny's eyes looked first to Alpert and then to Comey.

They both shook their heads.

"Fort Worth wanted a Black drover. I wanted a job."

The other interviews went about the same. Alpert and Comey talked to Tim next. After work, he fetched the beer from his truck. While he was out, he looked in on the animals. They were bedding down and everything seemed normal. The crew knocked back a couple. Then Billy moseyed down to the livestock pens. He came back wide-eyed and screaming. Tim couldn't remember ever seeing somebody so excited. It was almost unnatural. They all ran down to the barn. The drovers didn't search it long. It was easy to see that a one-ton side of beef was missing. Tim thought of the security footage. While Sarah and Destiny went to look at the tape, Billy went north in search of the roaming steer and Tim went south. Everyone ultimately met back at the office. Sarah then called the police and their boss.

"How'd you end up as a drover?"

"Graduated from college with a theater degree—acting, set design, that sort of thing. Westerns are having a bit of a renaissance at the moment. I needed a job, and I thought this one might give me some cred at a casting call."

"Anything else?" Alpert asked.

"Want to know what I think happened to Blue?"

"Tell me."

"One of those Silicon Valley transplants. Some vegan liberals from the Left Coast. They got no problem wearing leather shoes or pants. Ever try to make designer clothes out of broccoli? But a guy tries to eat a steak and they go wild-eyed crazy. I think they took Blue as some sort of protest. They got the skills to mess up our video."

"You got some sort of ransom note or anything to back up your theory?" Alpert asked.

Tim shook his head. "That's just what my gut says."

"Thank you and your gut for your input," Comey said.

Billy told the detectives about discovering that Blue had been rustled. While they were drinking, he'd discovered that he was missing his hat. At first, he figured that Tim had hidden it, then remembered that he'd taken it off while getting the cattle into their pens. He walked down to the barn.

"You know how you have this delayed reaction sometimes," he said.

Comey nodded.

"I walked by Blue's pen. Took a few steps, almost reached my hat, and it hit me that Blue wasn't there. I pulled on his gate. Then hauled ass back up to the office. Everybody ran down to see. Somebody, Destiny maybe, said we should check out the security tape. The girls ran back to the office. Tim sent me up the street. He thought Blue might naturally start walking toward the pasture. He ran the other way."

It was Alpert's turn to nod. "How'd you end up as a drover?"

"I grew up in West Texas. My family raises cattle. Our spread is small by West Texas standards, but we like it. Got kicked in the head by an old bull on Daddy's ranch. This herd's too tame to do something like that."

Alpert nodded again.

Alpert reinterviewed Sarah after the detectives had finished talking to the others. "You told me that Tim was your techie?"

Sarah nodded.

"How come he didn't look at the video with you and Destiny?"

"He did later. We went back to watch while the guys searched the streets," Sarah said.

"And when did you call the police?"

"After we all got back to the office."

Alpert leaned forward, narrowing the gap separating them. "Why'd you wait?"

"It just seemed like Blue had wandered off. My first thought wasn't a cattle rustler in the middle of Fort Worth."

"Billy told us a theory about what he thinks happened," Comey said.

Sarah laughed. "We've all got ideas."

"What's yours?"

"Pop-up restaurant."

Alpert looked at Comey. They both turned back to Sarah.

"They're a big deal in hip foodie circles." Her eyes flitted between the two of them.

"We're more the chicken-fried set," Alpert said.

Sarah nodded, apparently pleased with the answer. "Internet buzz begins with rumors of a secret restaurant opening temporarily at some undisclosed location. Got to be an A-lister to know where to go. Big price tag. Star chef. Gourmet meal. The ultra-fashionable thing to do. Then the restaurant disappears. A few months later, another one pops up."

"And you think Blue's on the menu?" Alpert began to ask.

"How edgy would it be to eat a celebrity? It's a meal, it's performance art. It'd be like Banksy shredding that painting just after it sold for a million bucks."

Alpert looked back to Comey. His lips formed the unspoken words, "what's a Banksy?"

Comey shrugged.

"Want to know the funny thing about that?" Sarah asked.

"I'd love to hear funny," Alpert said.

"Aged beef doesn't mean it comes from old cattle. The meat from a steer like Blue would be tough as leather. Any butcher would tell you that good steaks come from younger animals. If some pop-up stages a celebrity slaughter, I hope the customers have strong teeth and wine, lots of wine." She paused a moment. "Actually, I hope they break every tooth in their rich mouths and then choke on the gristle."

● ● ●

Alpert kicked off his shoes before he crossed the threshold into his house. He had no idea what he might have stepped in today, and he didn't want to track it inside. Back at the station, he'd had another pointed conversation with the lieutenant. The mayor had a press conference scheduled for tomorrow. The message was clear: deliver results or Alpert would be driving a patrol car on the midnight shift. The lieutenant had then stomped away. Alpert was pretty certain he'd seen the man grinning.

On the way home Brittney had called. She'd told him that although she'd had fun last night, she wasn't ready yet for anything serious. Too soon after the divorce. And she just didn't think she could date a cop. "It's not you, it's me," she'd said at the end.

Dumped by cliché, Alpert wished he'd let the call go to voicemail. He might have played the message for the lieutenant and solved one of the problems plaguing him.

The other problem, Blue's disappearance, still hung there like a side of beef.

Alpert fixed himself a seltzer and soda—on weeknights he skipped the Scotch—and collapsed on his couch. He spread his interview notes across the coffee table. He didn't look at them. Instead, he sipped his seltzer and thought about the last twenty-four hours and how they'd gone completely off the rails.

He should have stayed home last night and read a book. Instead, he'd gone drinking and overlooked all the warning signals. He'd listened to Jim Beam and ended up with a hangover, an angry boss, a career in peril, and a case he couldn't solve. Drinking made him miss the signs.

Alpert shook his head. He blamed those damn leather pants. He'd been watching those when his mind should have been focused elsewhere. But Jim had convinced him to look and now he had a case where his only hope was that the steer, in Comey's words, might magically reappear tomorrow. He sipped his club soda. The lieutenant was right, the mayor would not like to say the word *magic* when speaking to the press corps.

His eyes widened. "Magic," he said the word out loud.

Alpert sat up straight. He set down his glass and flipped through his notes and pictures.

Detective Alpert walked out of the cattle barn the next morning as the unmarked police car arrived.

Comey climbed out of the driver's side. The passenger door opened. Alpert had asked his partner to bring the lieutenant along to the north side.

Comey's mustache fluttered. "He ain't happy."

"What's this all about?" the lieutenant asked.

"Following up on a clue," Alpert said. He led them into the cattle barn. The drovers were all present. Sarah and Billy stood. Tim and Destiny were seated on the top rail of Blue's pen. The cattle in the barn paid little to no attention.

"How do you make a longhorn steer disappear?" Alpert asked.

Nobody answered. The lieutenant pulled out his phone and started checking his messages.

"Put it where it's not supposed to be." Alpert walked from Blue's pen to an empty enclosure across the central aisle. "If you put Blue here, he wouldn't be there." Alpert pointed at Blue's pen.

The lieutenant coughed.

"Every day these animals get paraded down the street. Walking Blue from one pen to another would take moments. Less time than the most basic errand, like checking a horse's leg. Wouldn't you agree, Destiny?"

She nodded from her perch atop the rail.

"Or retrieving a case of beer, Tim?"

"I guess," Tim said.

"But we checked the entire barn before we called the police," Sarah said.

"Everybody looked the barn over after they'd been drinking. Everybody searched while panicking to find their lost celebrity. Alcohol makes us miss things we'd normally pick up on. We don't use our most reasoned judgment after drinking. I know this as well as anyone." Alpert shot a glance. The lieutenant's eyes remained on his phone.

Billy pointed at the pen where Alpert stood. "I might miss a few things, but there's no way I'd miss seeing Blue if he were standing over there."

The rest of the drovers murmured agreement.

"What you missed," Alpert said, "was a foreshortened pen."

Billy cocked his head, confusion written on his face.

Alpert walked into the empty pen. He stopped near the back. "If I hung a screen here and put Blue behind it, you'd likely notice that the pen was shorter than normal. But if I plied you with alcohol and made you rush, you could easily fail to notice."

"I'd have noticed a screen," Billy said.

"Tim, if I took a picture of this back wall, could computer software print me up a backdrop that looked just like it?"

Tim shrugged. "I don't know."

Alpert grunted a laugh. "Sure you do. You majored in set design. Yesterday, there was a piece of PVC pipe hanging here. That held the backdrop."

Even the lieutenant's eyes traveled to the rafters above the pen.

"It's gone now," Alpert continued. "But Destiny helped me access last night's security video. We watched you carry it out of here after the place emptied."

Destiny nodded.

Tim looked at the group. "You can't believe…"

"Kids put sticky hands on Blue all day long. You knew that longhorn would just stand still during all the commotion."

"Sarah, you can't believe this," Tim said.

"Clever plan," Alpert said. "Blue follows you over here to this pen. Then you wait for someone to notice him missing. You supply the beer and stir things up. If anyone discovered your plan, your reputation as a practical joker would get you off the hook for the price of a case of beer. Then, you sent Billy toward the pasture and the women to watch the security video. The video can't record and play at the same time. With the security cameras stopped, you could just walk Blue out to a waiting livestock trailer. The traffic division pulled last night's video from the red-light camera down the street. We've got a license plate on the likely pickup. The truck registers to your brother."

The lieutenant pocketed his phone.

"It costs money for an actor to live in Hollywood. A quick sale of a prize steer would raise easy cash," Alpert said as Comey applied the handcuffs to Tim. "You were too quick to blame the Californians. Showed where your head was."

* * *

Comey turned the prisoner over to a uniformed patrol officer. The remaining drovers quickly disappeared without the use of magic, leaving the three detectives standing in the middle of the barn.

"Lieutenant," Alpert said, "Comey and I need to talk to Tim's brother about where he stashed Blue." He glanced at his phone. "If we leave now, we can likely have the steer recovered by the time the mayor holds her press conference."

"She'd like that," the lieutenant said.

"I was hoping that you'd have time to brief her on the status of the case. The mayor would probably like to display a police presence when she talks to the press."

The lieutenant frowned and dipped his chin. Then, he nodded. "That sounds like an excellent division of responsibility." He reached out and shook Alpert's hand. "Good work, Detective."

"It's what Major Case does, sir."

"How did you figure out about the screen?"

"When Comey mentioned 'disappear by magic,' it got me thinking about how you'd make an animal vanish onstage." He paused. "When Comey speaks, there's usually wisdom to be found, even when he don't know it. Jim Beam's reminded me recently to only listen to the voices I can trust."

MARK THIELMAN is a criminal magistrate working in Fort Worth, Texas. Formerly, he spent twenty-seven years as a prosecutor for Tarrant and Dallas counties. A two-time Black Orchid Award-winning novella author, Mark's short fiction has been published in *Alfred Hitchcock's Mystery Magazine*, *Black Cat Weekly, Mystery Magazine*, and various anthologies. He lives in Fort Worth with his wife, two sons, and an oversized dog. Learn more at MarkThielman.com .

RISK REDUCTION

By L. A. Starks

I make my living reducing risk for Pacer Insurance Company. "We're glad you could join us," my boss said nearly an hour ago. He'd stood with his arm wrapped around his girlfriend's waist as we talked in their kitchen.

"Thanks for inviting me."

Artie, my boss, had winked while Dena took my hand and stroked it.

It had been time to reduce my own risk.

● ● ●

I thought I'd landed a great job when I'd been hired at Pacer during my last semester of college, with the job set to begin after graduation. I loved my field (actuarial science—a fancy name for risk accounting). And the salary would enable me to cover the rent of my first apartment, which my chubby three-year-old son, Cody, and I had recently moved into, after living throughout college with my parents. (Cody's father? Not worth thinking about. He's out of the picture.)

When I started work, I got my group assignment. My boss would be Artie. I had assumed everyone sitting in my new-hire class in Pacer's large conference room knew as little as I did about our supervisors, at least until I talked to a guy sitting next to me, Ben. He appeared to have grown a beard to look older. Hadn't worked.

"You're with me in Artie's group?" Ben's tone was concerned.

"Yeah," I said. "Why?"

He leaned close and whispered. "I heard his group loses a few each year. Everyone gets good promotions, if they last, but that's a big if. He's cutthroat. Ranks people. The ones with the worst reviews either lose their jobs or are shipped off to North Podunk, Wyoming. I've heard people sometimes turn it around after they make his shit list, but not many."

Great. I turned my attention back to the speaker up front. And I'd been so excited about my new job. But still, I wasn't concerned. I was a hard worker, and I'd do whatever it took to succeed.

● ● ●

When I arrived that night at my parents' two-story home in Munger Place, Cody was staring out the front window, waiting for me. He looked like he'd had a good day with my mom. She and a babysitter were going to alternate taking care of him during the week.

"Look at you, precious boy!" I wrapped my chubby son in a hug.

"*Olá,*" my mother greeted me in Portuguese. "He's talking so much." Her long, pointed nose crinkled with delight. "Maybe even this weekend, you will finally hear all his new words."

I lifted Cody so his face was level with mine. "Who's Momma's best boy? Who?"

"Me!" A big, beautiful grin split his face. I felt the immense love for him I'd known even from the apprehensive earliest days of pregnancy.

"How was your first day?" my mother asked.

"Good." Mostly.

Before I packed Cody up for home, I told Mom a little about the presentations I'd heard and the group I'd been assigned to. But I didn't tell her what Ben had said about our new boss. No need to worry her or Dad. I'd simply apply myself and become one of Artie's success stories with the big promotion. I had my parents to thank.

"Mom, I wouldn't have this job, or maybe even a healthy son, without all the help you and Dad have given me. The financial support over the years—and I know you couldn't afford it--has meant a great deal. So does all the time you spent just listening to me while I figured out my life. And Cody's."

Mom smiled and shook her glossy black hair. "It's a pleasure. As you are learning with your own son, motherhood—being a parent—means sacrifice."

I lifted Cody to my hip and prepared to leave. "Love you!"

"Love you back!" Mom said.

The next day, seated in a smaller conference room, the six of us assigned to Artie's group met each other. I was glad to see Ben's friendly face.

My new boss was tall, barrel-chested, and charming.

We introduced ourselves. To me Artie said, "Allyson Ferreira. You grew up here in Dallas?"

"Yes. My family's Brazilian, but we've lived here for generations. I recently graduated from UTD," I said, referring to the University of Texas at Dallas.

"Where'd you go to school before that?"

I forced a smile, even though I hated the question. Everyone else in my starter class seemed to radiate money, as if they'd been born signed up for private school. Not me. "I went to DISD public schools." The Dallas Independent School District. It wasn't terrible, but it's not a school system people rave about. I quickly tried to change the subject. "My parents own Ferreira Auto Repair near downtown."

He laughed. "I know that shop. My car is there often."

I laughed back. "Well, maybe I can get you a discount."

"I need it."

As Artie moved on to the woman sitting beside me, I thought how relieved I was that Artie must know my dad. Maybe it'd work in my favor.

* * *

Our new-hire class finished the week with a mixer at Lekka. The Far North Dallas restaurant was near both private schools and highly rated public ones, something my parents hadn't been able to afford for me. Not Greenhill, Hockaday, or Ursuline, nor the suburban schools in Carrollton and Park Cities. I got out of my old Honda and smoothed my dress, determined to look like I fit in, even though it wasn't as fashionable as what the other women were wearing.

When Artie pulled his flashy orange Jaguar into the circle drive, the valets nearly came to blows over who would park it. A raven-haired woman, maybe thirty years old, exited from the passenger door. She wore a tight silk blouse, latex leggings, and gold bracelets that cost more than I would earn in the next year, even with a promotion. I followed her and Artie inside.

Lekka's patio was a pleasant, unhurried spot. Artie introduced his stunning girlfriend, Dena, to all of us. In what I perceived as kind focus, she asked me questions about growing up in Dallas and how I was adapting to the job. She wanted to know all about Cody. She didn't seem to care that I hadn't been born into money, like so many others, or that I was a single parent. She flashed me an enormous smile as she turned away to speak to Ben.

* * *

Dallas has many prosperous neighborhoods, but I'd grown up in a poorer one. My parents had relied on discount stores for my clothes when I was a kid. Now these low-cost shops met my need for the cheap pants and shirts Cody kept outgrowing. I was grateful the stores enabled me to keep my costs down, because I needed to help my parents, considering how much they'd helped me over the years and were still helping me with Cody. I'd worked part-time as a waitress in college, trying to contribute as much as I could to our household. Now that I was on my own and working full-time, I needed to do more for them.

That weekend my parents joined us at our apartment for breakfast, and I tried to give my mother money for that week's babysitting.

"*Não*. Family helps family."

"That's what I'm doing, Mom. Family helping family."

She shook her head.

"Mom, I see how much the electric bill has gone up."

She tried to refuse, but I squeezed the cash into her hand.

I set down plates of scrambled eggs, muffins, and a bowl of fruit salad and invited my parents to the table. Cody squealed with delight when I gave him a box of his favorite fruit juice.

I asked about Artie's car. My mother managed accounting for the shop and remembered he was a "good customer," which meant expensive bills paid on time. But she hadn't appreciated that he always kept a loaded gun in his glove box. My father recalled that despite the Jaguar's low mileage, Artie had driven too hard. "Tires wearing out too fast. He's new to us, just the last few months, so it's not a vehicle you ever worked on yourself."

Throughout high school and parts of college, I had spent evenings and weekends at the garage, checking in customers, paying vendors, and best of all, actually repairing cars. At first, I'd hid my greasy cuticles when I saw the painted nails of my female classmates, but later I displayed them with pride. I liked that I knew my way around the garage, even if I wouldn't want my new work associates to know it. Sure, I should be proud of myself around them, like I'd eventually been around my classmates in high school and college, but I was a work in progress.

In actuarial science, the main idea is the law of large numbers: we can price risks correctly given a big enough population and sufficient data. We worked at computers figuring out questions such as how many automobile accidents had happened in Houston in each of the last five Octobers. (Short answer: hundreds.) But as I was to learn, no such smoothing law applied to small numbers: two like me and Cody, or two like Artie and his girlfriend.

Soon, Artie sent me on the road, traveling from Dallas to client offices in Chattanooga, Oklahoma City, and Beaumont. After Cody came down with ear infections three weeks in a row, my mother took over his care full-time. She reported his activities to me every day when we video-chatted and made sure he always talked to me too.

I compiled statistics for loss modeling on epidemics, tornadoes, and hurricanes. How much money should Pacer set aside to pay for these future events, which were sort of predictable and sort of random? The work was complex and fascinating.

But each week I missed Cody more profoundly. His smiles and hugs were the world to me, yet every Monday I had to deep-freeze my love for him when I boarded an airplane.

"Desculpa." Sorry. Every Thursday evening, I apologized to my parents for my lateness in picking up Cody when my flights back to Dallas were delayed. I cried when the two of us finally entered our own stuffy apartment.

Then, despite my mother's constant care, Cody got the flu. He vomited so much she and my father had to rush him to the emergency room at Children's Medical Center. I was in Amarillo. I called every half hour, desperate to hear about him.

Finally, at two a.m., she texted me to say they were all back home and Cody was asleep.

Thursday night when I arrived, Cody shied away and grabbed my mother's legs with his hands. "No. Don't wanna go."

My heart broke.

The next two nights I barely slept. I liked being able to pay my bills, but not at the cost of my relationship with my three-year-old.

I called Artie on Sunday, trying not to sound as anxious as I felt. "I need projects that allow me to stay in Dallas. Cody's been getting sick, and I need to be here for him." I didn't add, *and I'm missing him like crazy and he's more attached to my mother than to me.*

"There will be a price. I expect people in your position to travel, so you won't advance as fast if you don't get on the airplane. Come by and see me tomorrow."

What I heard was that a compromise was possible. I was willing to try anything.

● ● ●

The early weeks of the new schedule in which I worked in Dallas and was home each night with Cody were a dream. The projects were more boring than our off-site projects and they carried into the weekend. But I was happy to make the trade.

On a few occasions, Artie gave me exasperated glances. Twice he asked, "Are you sure about your answers?"

The second time, I looked over the summary page in his hand. The totals were different from what I'd calculated. Yet the summary page was formatted—looked just like—the one I had given him. "These totals are reversed, which would lead to the exact opposite conclusion of the one I presented."

"Yet this is what you handed in."

I was concerned about confronting my new boss, but my integrity—my capability—was more important. "That's not what I gave you."

I was baffled. Had someone created a new summary page and substituted it to make me look bad? Had Artie?

He continued as if he hadn't heard me. "I'm worried, Allyson. If we make the wrong decisions because *you* slip up on the numbers, it not only costs Pacer Insurance money, but it could also cost people their lives."

"I understand, but I swear, the summary page is not the one I sent you."

He looked concerned, then shook his head.

I took a picture of the summary page with my phone's camera and later compared it with my own computer spreadsheets and summary page. The ones I had sent him. My table totals were correct—and the reverse of what he had showed me.

The next day I explained that my records showed the right numbers.

"So how do you justify the ones on my summary page?" Artie asked.

I couldn't.

On Fridays the six of us in the new-hire group went out with Artie and his girlfriend. That Friday, others had finished quarterly projects in Sacramento and Chicago, so we celebrated with extra drinks at Chilaquiles, an upscale neighborhood bar also known for its eponymous dish of tortilla chips, salsa, scrambled eggs, beans, crema, and cheese.

Chilaquiles was a vast, crowded serve-yourself space, so Dena took everyone's orders for the first round, and then after we'd toasted our early weeks, a second round. Each time, my drink was the only one with a blue umbrella—the others had orange and pink and green.

As she gave me my first drink she said, "Blue umbrella, to match your cute navy blouse."

The conversation progressed in fits and starts—we were all still new to one another. Suddenly, Dena's voice rose. "I can't believe you haven't told them who I am."

"You mean the part about being related to a New Jersey mobster?" Artie said. He smiled, but this appeared to be a familiar argument.

Dena didn't smile back. "No, the part about how I come from an important family and my parents have paid for everything—our house, that car. It sure as hell isn't your money."

Artie looked around at all of us, a pained smile. "Maybe we all need to slow down on the drinks."

"You talking about me again?" Dena's voice snarled.

Artie's tone could not have been more even-keeled. "No, Dena. All of us."

After an hour, as my colleagues rose to leave, I did too, thinking about what Cody and I would do on the weekend. Artie said, "Allyson, could you stay a minute?"

"Sure." A warning tone buzzed in my brain. Yet I was feeling sleepy too, with a headache starting. *What's this? Too soon for a hangover.*

Ben raised his eyebrows and silently signaled to me, *Call.*

After everyone else left, Artie leaned back and said, "Let's have another drink. Dena's getting them. You'll have to try our favorite."

Dena soon returned with icy rum-and-sodas.

"My favorite too," I said. "But I have a special recipe. I'll make it for you sometime." I was having trouble getting the words out.

Dena gave me her wide smile, in slow motion. "Awesome."

Artie's tone had suggested unwelcome news. I swallowed half my drink and waited.

"Allyson, there is no easy way to say this. Your work has been subpar. If it doesn't improve, I'll have to let you go."

"What?" Tired as I was, fear and anger started to war within me. I downed the rest of my drink to gain time. "I have done a hundred percent of everything you've asked, on deadline. I've worked late and weekends, as you know because you can see when I'm logged in. You've never said a word."

"I did. Remember the reversed table you gave me, which could have led to the exact wrong conclusion and at least a half-million-dollar mistake?"

"And remember I told you I had given you the correct summary sheet? Yet somehow you had one that was completely reversed."

"No. I don't remember. I don't think you did."

My eyes got wet. Artie's and Dena's faces blurred.

He tightened his lips in a sneer I had not seen before. "Is this a new effort at workshopping your feelings, Allyson? Try out tears, see how we react?"

"No!" But I felt weird, simultaneously mad and fuzzy.

And *ready.* I'd never thought of Artie this way before, but I wanted to go to bed with him *now.* I moved to sit next to him and slowly licked my lips.

Dena said, "Atta girl." She rubbed my neck and shoulders. "Sorry for the bad news. You shouldn't be driving. We'll take you home. Or do you want to stop by our house?"

The idea of being in Artie's house, near his bed, was tempting. But he was my boss, and he had a girlfriend. "No. I need to get my son."

"I'm sure you can figure out how to fix the problem," Artie said.

We climbed into the orange Jaguar. Dena sat in the back seat with me. I gave Artie directions.

We'd been driving for fifteen minutes when I realized we weren't going toward my parents' house.

"Where are we going? I said I need to get to my son."

"Are you sure?" Dena asked. "It's early enough to come to our place for a nightcap."

I thought about getting it on with Artie in a bathroom at his house while Dena made drinks. I had a feeling he'd be interested. But no. I had to get to Cody. It wouldn't be right to leave him in my parents' care for a couple more hours just so I could have fun.

"I'm sure," I said.

Artie changed directions, and when we were a few blocks from my parents' place, I said, "The house next to Ferreira's Auto Repair."

"Yes, I know the shop well," he said. "Your parents do a shit job on this car. Maybe if they got sued for negligence, they would clean up their act." His sly look in the rearview mirror told me everything about his power over me and my parents.

"My parents are honest!" *Aren't they? Damn this booze.*

Dena slid her hand up my skirt. I tried not to react.

"A relationship between three people can be fun, and so *rewarding* for everyone," she whispered. "Artie says you're Brazilian. You have that baby so you've got those big hot breasts. You should try it out with us."

A threesome? I couldn't sort my feelings—I was still ready to have sex right then—but as Artie parked the Jaguar in front of my parents' house I slid across the back seat, away from Dena. She followed me out of the car. For a moment I was afraid she would pursue me onto the lawn, but instead she stepped into the front passenger's seat of the gleaming orange Jag.

My mother must have been watching. She opened the door before I could knock. "Your boss Artie? I recognize the car."

"And his girlfriend. I had too much to drink so they brought me home."

"You should have texted us for a ride."

"Didn't think." I *had* had too much. *But why do I feel different from the slow haze I usually have when I drink?* "Where's Cody?"

"In the back with your father. Rinse out your mouth first. You want corned beef hash? We have leftovers."

"Yes. But I want to see Cody." I went to the bathroom, swirled strange-tasting mouthwash, and spat it out. I felt dizzy, restless. Afraid. *I could lose my job! Damn.* I resolved not to cry. Not here.

In the guest bedroom, my father and Cody showed me their wooden block projects and Cody tried out his newest dinosaur knowledge. "Momma! T. rex!"

"Fierce." I hugged him, glad to be with him, glad he was well. I was still paying bills from the emergency room trip. *What if he gets sick again and I don't have a job?*

After a few hours I was sober.

"Obrigada!" Thank you, I told my parents when they parked next to my Honda. Then I buckled Cody into his car seat and drove the two of us to our apartment.

After I put Cody to bed, I called Ben.

"How are you feeling?" he asked.

I wasn't sure how much to tell him. He was friendly, but he was a competitor.

Suddenly I was sobbing. "Artie threatened to fire me. Ben, I swear, I've been doing everything right. I triple-check my numbers."

"Is it because you're not traveling?"

"He said I was screwing up projects. He showed me results he says I gave him, but I didn't. I'm having trouble remembering everything that happened tonight."

"I've heard about his—sabotage before. Allyson, tell me what happened. Then write it all down."

"Why?"

"I'll explain. But first tell me what happened."

"You and the others left. I was already feeling woozy, odd. Different than I usually do when I drink. Artie asked me to stay for a few minutes. Dena brought us another round of drinks. Rum and soda." I sniffled.

"Did you see them being made? Or your earlier drinks?"

The bar had been out of my line of sight. "No. Why?"

"You wouldn't be the first person who had her drinks roofied. Could be the reason for your trouble remembering."

"Jesus. Why would she do that?"

"Artie and Dena look for people they think are powerless. Did they proposition you?"

My face flushed. I was glad our call was not on video.

"You don't have to give me details," Ben said. "But they have come on to Artie's new hires before. That's why everyone prefers to be on the road instead of in the office, near him. He, and I am guessing his girlfriend too, have figured out you need your job so much they can take advantage of you."

"Ben, how do you know all this?"

"Grapevine's powerful."

"Why didn't you tell me this before?"

His sigh was audible. "I should have. I didn't know if the gossip was true. Not for sure. I didn't want to badmouth my boss—*our* boss—in case it wasn't."

I didn't like it, but I could understand it. "Okay. I guess I should go to Human Capital. Please don't tell anyone I called." *Human Capital* was Pacer's name for human resources.

"I won't tell. But I'd be surprised if Human Capital helps. Big companies always circle the wagons when things like this happen."

We hung up. As Ben suggested, I wrote down everything. Already, pieces of the evening were disappearing from my memory.

I climbed into bed. Tossed and turned. The mathematics, statistics, and financial theory I applied to pension reserves or trends in tornado damage couldn't be applied to the problem of Artie's raw power. There was no logical answer because none of the outcomes were reasonable.

I looked up rohypnol and was scared to realize Ben was right—Dena had likely put it in my drink—the one with the blue umbrella, the one she said matched my shirt. That explained my bewildering attraction to Artie, which now horrified me.

The next moment I was furious. Like a good actuary, Artie had calculated the risk and decided there wasn't any. They had prepped me with rohypnol. Dena had proposed a threesome. Only my rush to get to my son had saved me. *This time.*

I finally fell asleep around three. Cody and I did Saturday chores, but my mind kept turning to the catastrophe my job had become. By Sunday evening I was desperate. Rage over my lack of power made my head hurt.

I'm angry enough to strangle them with my bare hands in a dark alley.

Reason surfaced. Artie and Dena didn't frequent dark alleys. I was not strong enough to take on two people. And alleys were monitored with cameras, anyway.

I could look for a position at another company. But at my entry level, Pacer was paying a lot more than I could earn anywhere else in town. I'd received other offers that paid less, with worse benefits, and seemed to be simply tabulations a high school graduate could do. The work at Pacer drew me in, made me think strategically. Maybe I could find another good job if I moved away, but there was no other place I wanted to live. I had grown up in Dallas. My parents—Cody's grandparents—were here.

Hoping for some peace, I took Cody to an Episcopal church for Evensong. We ducked into the back pew. Serenity flowed into my bones from each note of the choir's canticles. I felt safe, and realized I needed more of these feelings of safety and serenity in my life, something I would never get while working for Artie.

We sat through half the service before Cody got restless. Then we left.

As I put Cody to bed, realizing in just a few hours I'd have to face Artie, I became angry and humiliated all over again. With an effort, I switched off those feelings to consider my options and their cost-benefit analyses.

Artie and his girlfriend were threatening me, my son, and my parents. They'd identified me as poor and vulnerable. Other jobs I could get paid far less, and my family needed the money I made. And what kind of ugly or non-reference would Artie and the company be likely to give me?

A lawsuit would take too long, would be "she said–they said," and too hard to prove, if I even could win. And so much for working again in this risk-analysis field I loved. I would have become the big risk.

What if an accident killed Artie and Dena? The idea came unbidden, as if a devil on my shoulder had whispered it in my ear. Once in my mind, I couldn't discard it.

Between assisting my father with repairs and now my projects reviewing auto accidents, I had seen everything that could happen to a car. Especially a Jaguar driven fast.

I could loosen the Jag's tie-rod the next time it was in my parents' shop. The tie-rod connected the steering rack to the front wheels: a steering failure could lead to a fatal crash.

But if Artie and Dena were killed, forensics would trace the "adjustment" back to me, or worse, to my parents' shop. They didn't deserve the accusations or damage to their reputation. I— or my dad—might even be charged with a crime. I'd heard of it happening. Criminally negligent homicide. Murder, even.

I needed another idea, so I researched further, learned some useful information, did a cost-benefit analysis, and decided.

Then I deleted my browser history.

Monday morning, I left my cubicle and walked with a determined look toward Pacer's Human Capital office, which was a few doors down from Artie's office, at the end of the hall. I caught his eye as I passed his open door, and he must have guessed where I was headed. He bolted in front of me. Some rohypnol victims can't remember anything that happened to them while under the influence, but some have partial amnesia. Artie must have correctly figured I fell in the latter group. How many other women had he tried to head off at the pass, fearing they'd also remembered what he'd done to them?

Leaning in, he whispered, "I wouldn't if I were you. I've already warned them. If you go to Human Capital, you'll never work again. Not here. Not anywhere. What will happen to your parents and son? You know, you could solve it all if you changed your mind and spent time with me and Dena."

Now that I understood Artie, I realized this was classic behavior for him. First he threatened me, then he played on my guilt about my family, and then he offered an out. He was a sadist.

I tilted my head as if confused and whispered back, "If I'm going to have a relationship with you and Dena, shouldn't Human Capital know about it?"

He stopped, surprised and wary. Then smiled wolfishly. "You don't need to tell Human Capital. Friday. Seven p.m. at our place."

On Friday night, Cody was safely with my parents. I told them I was going to dinner with my boss and his girlfriend, but that I had seen Artie and Dena argue before. If it happened again tonight, I would return early.

I stopped by the repair shop and took the items I required. I concealed everything in a tote and draped it across the front seat of my Honda.

Traffic cleared as I wound northwest. I'd worn my shortest outfit, a low-cut blue dress that buttoned in the front from top to bottom. Paired with high heels, it was a look my mother hated. "Wear that dress, you'll get pregnant again."

"Não entendi." Not following you. But of course, I had. I couldn't run in heels, so I would take them off if I needed to escape.

I drove into Artie and Dena's fancy subdivision. Where my parents lived, the houses were practically on top of one another. Here, the homes were so far apart, you could scream bloody murder and your neighbors wouldn't hear.

At the door of their big white boxy mansion, I clutched the tote. *This is crazy.* But I thought about Cody, and about Artie's threats against me and my family. *Family takes care of family.* I pushed the doorbell.

Dena answered the door not five seconds later and gazed approvingly at my dress and heels. "You look ready for fun!"

"Vamos! Let's go! It's Friday." I laughed. "You must have seen me arrive on your security camera."

"No camera. I was just near the door. Growing up in my family, you learn early on you don't want a record of who comes and goes."

Just as I'd hoped. I smiled while she waved me in.

As we walked through the living room, I draped my jacket over an arm of a big sofa. I placed the book I'd brought onto the coffee table nearby but kept my tote with me.

"Artie's in the kitchen," Dena said.

Artie was leaning against a capacious island surrounded by gray granite countertops and cupboards. His glance slid up and down my figure. He looked at Dena, and they smiled together.

"We made hors d'oeuvres!" Dena waved toward slabs of cheese, chopped vegetables, and what looked like candy. "Have indica gummies like we just did. Puts you in the chill mood."

"Later, definitely," I lied, pulling the rum from my tote— while thinking—*good*. Indica was a pain-reducer that might make them sleepy. "Show me where your glasses and a tray are."

Dena led me to a cabinet by the kitchen entrance. On the counter right below it was a bowl with two sets of keys, including a Jaguar key fob.

"So, Dena," I said, "last time we hung out you were interested in Brazil. I love it there. They have these amazing nude beaches. I left a book about them in your living room with lots of cool photos."

"I told you she was wild, Artie."

"Go take a look," I said. The pictures were explicit, showing much more beachgoer skin than bathing suits or sand. I unbuttoned the top button of my dress. "I'll finish up the drinks. Then we can relax."

Fortunately, they followed my suggestion. Both walked around the corner, out of sight. I grabbed three glasses and poured dark soda into them, much more into my glass than theirs. I added mint leaves to theirs, my version of Dena's blue umbrella. Then I pulled the large thermos from my tote and filled the mint-leaf glasses with its liquid. As a cover, I poured most of the rum down the sink instead of into any of the glasses.

I reached into the tote again and turned on my phone's recording app. There was no place in my tight dress to hide it, so I hoped our conversation would carry into the kitchen. I would have to coax them into raising their voices.

I put the doctored drinks on the tray and carried them into the living room—not spilling a single drop—while holding my own drink in my other hand. Who knew my waitress experience would be so useful? Artie and Dena were paging through the book.

"We're ready to go to these beaches!" Dena said.

I sat against her on the leather couch and unbuttoned another button. "Let's toast your beautiful home. Bottoms up."

They grinned, and we all drank.

Then Artie started staring at my chest. I needed to provoke them, distract them. I remembered their argument about money at Chilaquiles, before the evening had turned so horrible for me. "Your house must have cost a fortune. How much?" I asked.

"Too much." Dena frowned.

"But it's perfect for us," Artie replied.

"It's good to know Pacer Insurance pays so well," I said.

"It does," Artie said.

"Who are you kidding?" Dena said, raising her voice. "We own this house because of my money."

"You mean your father's money and our thirty-year mortgage." Artie was no longer smiling. His voice was louder too.

"Here we go again." Dena's voice had turned into a screech.

"If he wasn't such an asshole—" Artie began.

"If you weren't such an asshole, you wouldn't take his money." Dena was at full volume now.

"Oops. Sensitive subject. Another drink?" I asked.

I took their glasses.

Dena followed me into the kitchen. *She can't see what I'm doing!*

"The cheese and gummies." She picked up the tray and left.

I took a deep breath. Then I repeated my special cocktail for them, returning with fresh drinks.

"Tastes funny." Artie frowned.

Crud. He hadn't noticed that on the last round. I must have used less soda this time. "Coconut, mint, lime, and a locally made soda. And my favorite rum." I held my breath, hoping he'd believe me. He drank some more with a shrug. *Whew.*

He pushed a button and speakers thrummed a slow melody.

"That bass makes me feel so sexy," Dena said.

"Softer on the music," I said. "I want to hear what you're saying." *So does my phone in the kitchen.*

Artie turned down the volume. Then he moved onto the other side of the sofa so I was sandwiched between him and Dena. He unbuttoned my dress further.

Crap. I thought this stuff would kick in faster. I'd already poured each of them more than the maximum dose. They weren't reacting.

I turned to him. "So, you two have any plans for kids?"

"I want them. She doesn't." He reached beneath my bra and grabbed one of my breasts. I kept my face still.

Dena's expression hardened and her words slurred. "Always my faul'." She smiled lazily. "But you can make us feel better." She slipped her hand up my dress.

I'm running out of time! "Your parents must be ready for you to have children!"

"Say, Allyson. You look hot. You ever been tied up?" Dena asked.

Oh God. But I need her to repeat it for the recording. "What?"

"I say, have you ever been tied up?" Dena shouted. "Are you hard of hearing or something?"

"Yeah, a little. So where do your parents live?" My voice cracked with fear. I hoped they didn't notice.

"Hers in dumbshit snootyville," Artie mocked.

"And hizzzz in south slimeytown." Dena hiccuped. "C'mon Allyson. No more questions. Time for bed."

"Let me go!" I shouted as loud as I could for the phone recording. I squirmed away from their hands and jumped up, deliberately kicking the table and knocking over a glass. I lowered my voice to a whisper. "Just one more drink first?"

"Don't go." Dena grabbed the air after me.

"She our guesssst tonight. What she wants," Artie said to his girlfriend.

I desperately made a third round of drinks, theirs again with the old chartreuse-colored ethylene glycol, an antifreeze I'd appropriated from my parents' garage. Unlike today's antifreeze, which tasted bitter, this old formula tasted sweet.

"I can drink faster than you," I said softly when I brought in the tray. Faster was a challenge that always spurred Cody.

Them too, it appeared. They downed their drinks.

Finally, they fell sideways, away from one another. They dozed, as unconscious as if I had given them fifteen normal shots. They didn't stir when I screamed, "You're hurting me!"

Given the amount of antifreeze they'd drunk, they could be dead within several hours, maybe a day—unless they woke up and start barfing. I needed to reduce my risk further.

I buttoned my dress, returned to the kitchen, placed the thermos in the tote, and turned off the recording app. I took the rum bottle into the living room. My tormentors were snoring, mouths open.

I poured some rum into Dena's mouth and stroked her throat to get her to swallow it. She did, not waking. I repeated the process with Artie. He stirred, then was silent. The autopsy results would show the alcohol in their bodies, which should help explain what supposedly happened next.

I slipped on gloves from my tote and wiped everything I had touched. I pressed the rum bottle against Artie's fingertips before leaving it on the gray countertop. Then I picked up Artie's key fob and retrieved his gun from his Jaguar's glove box. As expected, it was loaded. *Thank you, Mom, for mentioning it my first week of work.*

Back inside, I returned the key fob to its bowl, pulled on and zipped up my jacket, and eased beside Artie on the couch. With my hand in front of him, I shot Dena in the chest. Then I quickly put the gun against Artie's temple and pulled the trigger again. Fighting off nausea, I put the gun in his hand, making sure his fingers were on the grip and trigger, then I let it fall to the floor beside him.

If ever asked, I'd admit I was at Artie and Dena's tonight and would say their argument had escalated. That I had escaped after they threatened to tie me up. I had the recording. I'd say I made it to prove to Human Capital that my boss had been behaving inappropriately, and I'd been too afraid to come forward once their bodies were found.

But I hoped it wouldn't come to that. I hoped the police would think Artie and Dena had done themselves in, with no third party involved.

Murder–suicide? Artie shot Dena and then himself. *Tragic.*

I pushed my jacket inside a garbage bag I'd brought. I'd dump it in a closed business's trash bin on the way home. In the car, I'd use baby wipes to ensure I had no blood on me. That should do it.

I grabbed my book and the tote, ready to leave. As much as I could, I had eliminated the threat to Cody, me, and my parents. I stared at Artie's and Dena's bodies, their fashionable clothes, their house, and realized I no longer was intimidated by them or anyone else. They and other people at Pacer might be richer than me, but what I had was more important: my child, my parents, my job, and my life. I looked at them once more. They'd brought this on themselves. *"Adeus."*

Risk reduced.

Texan **L. A. STARKS** is the author of the award-winning Lynn Dayton thriller series: *13 Days: The Pythagoras Conspiracy*, *Strike Price*, and *The Second Law*, with a fourth underway for publication in 2023. *The Second Law* was an action/adventure finalist in the 2020 National Indie Excellence Awards and a mystery/thriller quarterfinalist in the 2019 BookLife Prize competition. One of her previously published stories, "Essence of Genius, Genius of Essence," won honorable mention in WOW!'s Spring 2021 Flash Fiction contest. She has a B.S. in engineering and an MBA. Besides writing high-stakes thrillers, she is a paid contributor to *Seeking Alpha* for her energy-investment articles and has run twenty half marathons. lastarksbooks.com

ROAD RAGE

By Pam McWilliams

Detective Abel was chain-smoking the cigarettes he'd given up for the woman he loved when he got the call about the road-rage killing on 75.

"Idiots," he said, extinguishing the burning butt in the overworked ashtray beside his bed. It was two a.m., but he was still on call.

"Gun?" he asked the dispatcher.

"Affirmative."

Road rage was all over the news these days, but it was hardly new. Sixteen years ago, his now ex-wife was involved in a road-rage incident that had wrecked their lives.

He put on a lightweight suit—too tight around his middle, damn it—and trudged out to his car. The temperature was hovering at 105. He blasted the air, but it didn't change anything. The world was still hot and miserable and so was he.

The incident was on the northbound side of 75, about five minutes from downtown. He took the Northwest Highway entrance and saw the flashing lights up ahead. A couple of police cruisers had blocked off the right lane to keep traffic away. At this hour on a Tuesday, there was much less than usual, but heat like this meant tempers were rising, among the hotheads in particular. And if alcohol was involved, ticked off could turn crazy in a heartbeat.

Abel pulled his car in behind all the other vehicles at the scene: the ambulance, a patrol car, a red Porsche, and a white Tesla. Both cars looked like showroom beauties that had gotten into a shoving match after leaving the lot.

He knew one of the two officers. Jeter. They greeted one another with the usual banter about the joys of being a cop on a night like this. The junior cop he didn't know, but the kid—he looked sixteen, for God's sake—was staring at him like he was a rock star. This hero shit was highly overrated. The problem was he knew who the real hero was, and she wasn't even talking to him.

Concentrate. The dead guy was already on a stretcher beside the ambulance. Abel walked over and pulled back the sheet. *Shit.* The victim was wearing a white cotton polo shirt, and the combination of too much blood and the metallic smell made him want to vomit. Max—God, how he missed her—she would have told him it was the cigarettes messing with his stomach and they'd kill him from cancer unless smoking in bed got him first. And in *that* case, he might also incinerate the firefighter who'd come to rescue him. He hated her husband, the fireman turned fire chief. Had Joe been the one to rescue Max when that sadist nearly killed her? No, he hadn't. Not that Abel didn't beat himself up on a regular basis for not finding her sooner.

"One shot, straight through the heart," the medic said. "Explains all the blood."

Abel took his word for it. He couldn't stomach looking at that blood-drenched shirt another second. He pulled up the sheet so that only the victim's face was showing. Midthirties, maybe. Full head of dark hair, slicked back like that basketball coach Pat Riley used to do back in the day. Except this guy had more hair. And a scar jutting out of his right eyebrow like the racing flag that gets lowered at the start of a race. A race to the death, as it turned out.

"Thanks, you can take him away," he told the medics.

He walked back to the two cops and said to Jeter, "Let me go talk to the lone survivor. What's his name?"

"Brad Crawford."

"Thanks. After, we can compare notes."

"The dead guy was Anthony Sanchez. He had a gun too but never got off a shot."

"Right," Abel said, grateful that Jeter had volunteered that information since he would have forgotten to ask. God, he was really losing it. Good thing most of these road-rage killings were routine. Two strangers get into a pissing contest on a highway, tempers flare, and one or both of them have a gun or maybe just a baseball bat. This was Abel's experience, but he wasn't about to assume anything. That's why they called him *detective*.

Crawford was sitting on the shoulder of the road behind the Tesla, head in hands. The Porsche was in front of the Tesla, at an angle that suggested its driver had cut off the Tesla.

"Mr. Crawford? I'm Detective Abel."

Crawford raised his head, then slowly rose. He was tall, a little taller than Abel, but not an ounce of fat on him. He didn't look perturbed in the least that he'd killed somebody, more like he'd spent a restless night trying to fall asleep. Abel should know since most of his nights were like that, although when he looked in the mirror, he didn't see a face like Crawford's. This guy looked about fifteen years younger—maybe thirty-two—and he was blond, with the good looks of a young Robert Redford. Abel made note of his Tommy Bahama shirt and khakis, worn with a pair of expensive loafers. He'd probably eaten his baby food with a gold-plated spoon and sailed into adulthood in a custom-made catamaran.

"Which car is yours?" Abel said.

"Tesla."

"Okay." Looked like he'd been the one who was cut off. "Tell me exactly how this happened."

"Maybe the guy was drunk, but he was going way too fast and—"

Abel interrupted. "Start at the beginning."

"I told the two officers," he said evenly. "Didn't they tell you?"

"No. I want to hear it from you."

"I was downtown with a client. We'd gone to a Rangers game out in Arlington and stopped at a bar in Dallas on the way home."

"So you'd been drinking."

"No!" he said, then backtracked. "Actually, I did have one beer at the start of the game. Nothing after. I was driving, after all."

"But postgame, you did go to a bar." Abel gave him a tight smile, and Crawford flushed.

"Ask them." He pointed to the two officers. "I passed their test."

"We'll get to that," Abel said. "Where's your friend?"

"My *client* lives downtown and said he'd Uber home. I live in Plano on the Frisco border, near where I work."

"Okay, now tell me who pissed who off."

"I saw the Porsche in my rearview mirror, coming up fast behind me in the right lane. There wasn't much traffic, so I slowed down, hoping the car would zoom past me in the middle lane. Instead, the guy rammed the back of my car, at which point he went ballistic and sideswiped me a few times, then cut me off. When he got out of his car, he had a gun. I grabbed mine. Thank God I did, because he told me to say my prayers since he was going to blow my head off. Next thing I knew, I'd shot him."

"Anthony Sanchez," Abel said. "Name ring a bell?"

"No."

Crawford said it a little too quickly. He should have thought about it, if only for a few seconds.

"One shot straight through the heart," Abel said, pointing to his own. The ache in his heart hadn't proved fatal, but it never went away. "Skill or luck?"

"You'd be hard-pressed to call it skill. I moved to Texas about a year ago and was told everyone should have a gun. Looks like they were right."

"You grow up hunting?"

Crawford shook his head.

"Spend much time at the shooting range?"

"A little. After I bought the gun. Kind of stupid if I didn't."

"You a Rangers fan?"

"More like a home-team kind of fan. Plus they were playing the Yankees."

"How many games you been to?" Abel asked.

"This was my first. Like I said, I haven't been in Texas all that long."

Abel asked him a few more questions, wrote down the answers, then closed his notebook.

"I'm going to let you go, but you'll have to report to the police station tomorrow morning and file a written statement."

"Should I bring a lawyer?"

"If you think you need one."

Crawford's eyes widened. Fear or surprise, Abel couldn't tell. He left him hanging and went to compare notes with Jeter and the kid.

Jeter explained that they'd arrived on the scene within five minutes of the shooting. Crawford was crouching next to the back of the Porsche, a couple of yards away from the body. Sanchez was clearly dead, although the medics arrived minutes later and confirmed.

"How did Crawford seem?" Abel asked.

"Not upset, exactly, more like shock. Maybe that's why he didn't attempt to help Sanchez."

Abel nodded. Crawford, he realized, didn't have a drop of blood on him and would have if he'd tried to administer any kind of first aid. As for the rest, Crawford had told Jeter and the kid the same basic facts he'd told Abel.

While they were talking, a news crew pulled up. Given the 24/7 news cycle, they seemed later than late. A cameraman and a reporter with a microphone jumped out of the SUV.

"Nothing to see here, guys," Abel told them. "Road rage kills. That's all your viewers need to know right now."

The reporter tried to get more out of him, but he just shook his head and walked away

The kid asked him, "You think there's anything fishy about this killing, Detective?"

"No idea. I got to do all the usual stuff before I arrive at 'fishy.'"

The kid looked disappointed. He must have thought the hero detective had a crystal ball for a brain.

Abel was at the station bright and early the next morning— easy peasy, since he couldn't sleep anyway. *Easy peasy* was a Max expression, now his. Even though thinking about her was another ping in his achy-breaky heart, he smiled and got to work.

The first phone call he made was to Crawford's ball-game buddy, Ron Dinkman. The guy was clearly hungover and had no idea Crawford had been involved in a road-rage killing after leaving the bar. He agreed to meet Abel at a coffee shop in Uptown, near Klyde Warren Park.

After they were seated, Abel filled him in on the shooting while Dinkman downed two cups of coffee.

"Man, I'm glad I wasn't there to see *that*." He looked young, maybe late-twenties.

"You own a gun?" Abel asked.

"Doesn't everyone?"

"I guess." Abel shook his head. "That's kind of the problem these days."

Dinkman said his company did business with Crawford's, and he'd first met him at a cocktail reception. "The guy's a real hotshot tech guy." He said he'd probably mentioned to Brad that he was a Rangers fan. And while Ron had his own season tickets, Brad had called and said he had two tickets behind home plate for the Yankees game. Dinkman jumped at the chance and sold his own ticket for a nice profit.

"Did Crawford drink much last night?"

"Hell, no. Had one beer at the game and didn't even finish it."

"Really?" he said, acting surprised.

"Said he had a big presentation today, so he had to keep it together. Plus, he said it wouldn't be too cool if he killed a client while driving drunk."

"No, it wouldn't. But he did kill a stranger while driving sober," Abel said. What he didn't say was, *Crawford had a big presentation today? Makes no sense he'd stay out that late.*

"Road rage seems like the last thing he'd get involved in," Dinkman said. "I mean, I don't know him real well, but the guy's super chill. Never even lost his cool when our guys made a stupid play, which happened a lot."

"Which is why you were drowning your sorrows at the bar after the game."

Dinkman chuckled, then winced and massaged his forehead. "That and Brad was paying."

"Paying but not drinking."

"Right."

"And he left before you?" Abel said. "Tell me about that."

"Nothing to tell. I remember he was saying something, and I was doing my best to pay attention, and he looks at his phone and says he didn't realize how late it was and he had that presentation in the morning. Could I get myself home? Uber's no problem, I told him, and he left."

      ● ● ●

When Abel got back to the station, Crawford was there—without a lawyer, he noted—giving his statement to Jeter and the kid. He left them to it and called Crawford's company and asked for him. His admin picked up. Abel identified himself and asked if she knew about the incident last night.

"Poor Brad," she said. "He feels terrible about it, but I keep thinking it could have been him who was killed. Thank God Brad had a gun."

Abel told her Crawford was here at the police station, giving his statement. And that he wasn't sure how much longer Crawford would be, so if he hadn't already rescheduled his big presentation, maybe she better do that?

"I'm not aware of one. Let me check his calendar."

Abel stayed on hold until she came back.

"I'm not seeing anything, but maybe it's something he rescheduled himself. Did he ask you to—?"

"That must be it," he said and thanked her for her time.

      ● ● ●

Abel needed to find any witnesses to the pissing contest between the Porsche and the Tesla or the shooting or both, so he asked the local TV station and *The Dallas Morning News* to ask their viewers and readers, and he posted something on the police department's Facebook page. He also conducted a bunch of interviews, including with the victim's neighbors, who described him as kind of full of himself, but basically a decent guy. No steady girlfriends or known enemies banging on his door. Both his parents were deceased, killed in a car accident of all things. By five p.m. Abel was whipped, and he was home and changed out of his work clothes when the doorbell rang an hour later.

Max was standing there with a covered casserole. With one beat of his achy-breaky heart, his exhaustion fell away. He stared rapturously at her face, her sun-yellow dress, and her bare arms and legs glistening from the heat, but he couldn't get out a single word.

"It's been a while," she acknowledged, meeting his gaze. She was never one to look away, even that last time when she decided she had to walk away.

He would have hugged her if not for that damn casserole. "Two years, ten months—"

"Saw you on the news."

"Up late?" He wondered if she and Joe watched TV in bed. Better that than—.

"Actually, it was on this morning's news. You didn't look so good, like you haven't been eating right."

"Come in, come in," he said. "It's too damn hot to stand outside."

"Only for a minute," she said, and he followed her into the kitchen. He didn't cook much, so it was mostly coffee cups in the sink, not totally disgusting.

"What kind of casserole?" he asked, even though he wanted to ask her other things. *Intimate* things.

"Most casseroles are comfort food that clog your arteries while packing on the pounds. *This* is a roast chicken with steamed green beans. You could probably get two or three meals out of it, depending on how hungry you are."

He was very hungry but not for food. "Homemade?" he asked, inching closer.

"Yes."

"God, Max, is there anything you're not good at?"

"Joe's a much better cook."

"*He* cooked this?"

"Calm down. I cooked it. Anyone who can read can cook. That's what I was about to say."

"I can read, but I can't cook."

"You're a special case."

"Special, huh?"

She smirked, even though he could tell she was trying not to.

He smirked right back. He had a killer smirk, and she had nowhere to go with her back up against the kitchen counter.

"You're smoking again." She frowned. "I can smell it."

He shrugged. "Work. It gets to me sometimes."

"Like with this road-rage killing, I imagine." Her expression turned empathetic.

Years ago, in the course of investigating a murder at Max's place of business, he'd told her about his wife. Ex-wife for a long time now, since right after they released her from prison.

"Yes, I mean no," he stammered. "Christ, I'm not going to lie to you, Max. I smoke because you're never in the room. Because you're the first person I think of when I wake up and the last person when I fall asleep. I only dream so I can dream of you."

The room got steamy all of a sudden, their breathing heavier, their chests rising and falling in sync. His gaze on hers, hers on his, everything in step and locked together except for their actual bodies. Beads of perspiration appeared on her forehead, and when she moistened her lips, it was the sexiest thing he'd ever seen. The only thing standing between them was the goddamn casserole. He was about to throw it across the room when she spoke.

"You know," she said gravely, never lowering her gaze, "Joe's not to blame for anything that happened. He's a good man. And things are much better between us, ever since you and I—well, you know."

At least she had the decency to blush. Then she told him how to reheat the food she'd brought—and left.

He lit a cigarette to fill the empty space, then poured himself a double scotch to dull the pain. He took both with him, stretched out on his bed, and let himself dream, even though he was wide awake.

She'd shown up at his house late on a stormy night about six months after he'd saved her from that monster. Her face was wet and not just from the rain.

"What's happened? Where's Joe?" he asked.

"Fire station."

"All this rain, fires should put themselves out."

"Do I seem different to you?" she said. "Do I look different?"

He didn't really know what she was getting at. "It's been a while, but—"

"I'm not a victim," she shouted. "And I refuse to live that way."

"Okay?"

"Joe's afraid to touch me, afraid of triggering bad memories. Or at least that's what he says. Does that make any sense, when that's the last thing I'd ever want?"

"Makes no sense to me."

"Why's that?"

"Well, for starters, I've seen you naked."

It wasn't the kind of thing he would have said if he'd planned ahead. "Uh, sorry." He stopped himself from saying more because it wasn't fair to tell her the whole truth. That he'd been half in love with her since before he'd rescued her from that demented drug lord.

She took a tentative step toward him, her eyes ravenous and a little crazed. He quickly closed the gap between them, and then they were kissing and tearing off each other's clothes and making love the way lovers do, lovers with a past, a present, and a future.

● ● ●

At work the next day, he read Crawford's statement, then had to read it a second time for the words to stick. He felt hungover, not from the booze, more like from Max's visit. He thought of that line from a Joni Mitchell song about putting ink on a pin beneath the skin to fill a void. It cheered him up. He wasn't the only sad sack in the world, and lots of people managed to put one foot in front of the other and keep going. Joni could probably tell him a thing or two about that.

Abel had his own office—ever since the powers that be decided he was "a hero"—and he was at his desk eating a late lunch when Jeter stopped by to discuss Crawford's statement.

Little things bothered him, he told Jeter. The fact that Crawford lied about having a big presentation the next morning.

"Could have been his escape plan," Jeter said. "Gave him an excuse to call it a night without offending his client."

"True. It's just that I talked to the bartender. Crawford told him to run an open tab and add a big tip and that if he ended up leaving before his buddy, he'd come get his credit card the next day."

"You're saying he got all his ducks in a row so he could leave at a moment's notice."

"Yes. And he did leave in a hurry," Abel said. "The thing is, without a connection between Crawford and Sanchez, there's no motive. And if this was some kind of premeditated crime, Crawford would've had to know that Sanchez was at another bar a half mile away and where he was headed when he left."

"Where *was* Sanchez headed?"

"The receipt for his bar tab was in his wallet. Sanchez was a regular there, especially after Rangers games, and the bartender remembered him and his friends calling it a night. Makes sense since bars close at two. Home was a condo on Walnut Hill, just off Seventy-five."

"What's next?" Jeter asked.

"I'm going to pay a call on the shooting range where Crawford learned to shoot."

Talking to the manager of the shooting range gave him nada.

"Yeah, I remember him." The manager handed back Crawford's photo. "Probably because he looked like that actor. Gosling. It sure as hell wasn't his shooting."

"Gosling?"

"Ryan Gosling, the movie star?"

"Oh, right," Abel said. "Guess I watch too many old movies. Anyway, this guy's shooting was *that* bad?"

"Why, what did he do?"

"I guess he got lucky," Abel said, but he didn't really believe it.

An hour later, he was sitting at his desk, waiting as an officer escorted the dead man's two drinking buddies, Mack and Jimmy, back to Abel's office. Usually, he'd speak with witnesses at their homes or workplaces, but these guys had asked if they could be interviewed at the police station ("we've never been inside one!"), saying it might help them wrap their heads around the fact their larger-than-life friend was really dead. *Killed!*

Abel thought they could pass for brothers. Dark-haired and muscular like their dead friend, but face-wise, they looked like kinder, less aggressive versions. They were obviously cut up over his death. "He was only thirty-three!" As were they. "We met freshman year at Texas Tech!" These days they worked hard, went to Rangers games, and raced dirt bikes on country roads or made the occasional trip to Vegas.

Abel asked them where their ball-game seats were— nowhere near Crawford's—and when asked if Tony had exchanged words or fists with anyone at the game, their answer was a resounding no.

Despite the loss to the Yankees, they said, Tony had been in high spirits. His business (liquor distributor) was going "insanely great" and he'd been about to close on an "amazing house in Preston Hollow for a cool one point six mil."

At thirty-three. Abel almost rolled his eyes. "Any girlfriends?" he asked.

"Two or three. Nobody serious."

"Yeah," Mack added, "but maybe he wanted to settle down. Why else buy a house like that?"

"Anybody who hated him that you know of?"

They didn't. He could be a bit of a hothead, they admitted, "but did he shoot anybody? He's the one who ended up dead."

"The name Brad Crawford ring any bells?"

They thought about it and shook their heads.

"A lot of alcohol in his system when he died," Abel said. "Probably affected his judgment, not to mention his gun handling."

The two friends strenuously disagreed, saying Tony could hold his liquor better than anyone they'd ever met.

● ● ●

Abel arrived home in a good mood. It definitely wasn't because of the case. It was Max. Since her unexpected visit, he'd had a bounce to his step and a mind that felt a whole lot sharper. She wouldn't have come to see him if she didn't still care. So when the doorbell rang at six-thirty, he wasn't surprised to see her. And this time she didn't come bearing food as an excuse.

"Welcome back." He grinned and opened the door wide.

"It's not what you think," she said, brushing past him.

Right.

She took a seat on a chair in the living room. He sat on the nearby sofa, imagining their bodies commingling before long.

"How's your road-rage case going?" she asked.

"It's going."

"I've got a client, a real-estate agent. We make her signs."

God, Max looked great. Her legs in that skirt, her dark hair brushing against the collar of her white blouse.

"People tell me things. Some things I wish they wouldn't. Anyway, she's worried."

Abel realized he needed to start paying attention to what she was saying, even if she was just using it as an excuse.

"Worried about what?" He gazed at her with desire.

"Brad, the guy who shot your road-rage victim. She's been dating him."

"Dating Brad or the dead guy?"

"Brad," she snapped. "Abel, pay attention."

"Sorry." He focused. "Well, tell her a woman *should* think twice before getting serious with a guy who's shot and killed somebody. Unless of course, he's a policeman."

Their eyes met, and he saw her expression soften.

"If only it were just that," she said.

He wondered how much worse it could be. "Tell me."

"This woman, she's also Brad's real-estate broker. That's how they met. He's been looking for a house. And together they found one, a real beauty from the sound of it." She paused and let out a deep breath. "Except he got outbid by somebody else."

No way, he told himself. It couldn't be a coincidence. That would be over-the-top crazy. "This house isn't in Preston Hollow, is it?"

"So you *do* know," she said.

"All I know is that the dead guy was about to close on a house in Preston Hollow."

"The listing agent for the house works at the same firm as my client. So, when the listing agent found out that Anthony Sanchez was dead, she notified her colleague. As the second-highest bidder, Brad Crawford was next in line to buy the house."

"Holy shit."

A lucky shot, huh? The next morning Abel made a list of all the shooting ranges within a limited radius of Crawford's apartment. The first three—nada. His fourth stop was a new place, open six months and a twenty-minute drive from Legacy West, home to Crawford's swanky, high-rise apartment building.

The Gold Star Gun Club had a circular drive with a valet. It looked like a country club for people who preferred a blood sport to golf and tennis—the kind of upscale place where someone like Crawford might feel right at home.

The manager wasn't particularly cooperative. Crawford's name didn't ring a bell, and he didn't recognize the photo Abel showed him.

"Look," Abel said. "I understand your position. People come here for fun or because they're hunters looking to up their game or they want to be able to defend themselves if the need arises. You don't want to scare off your customers by getting too cozy with the police."

"Owning a gun is a right," the manager huffed.

"Agreed. What I'm looking into here is strictly routine, which means I have to check all the boxes. Besides, Crawford told me this is where he learned to shoot. Do you really think—"

"Say no more." He turned to the computer on his desk. "Brad Crawford, you said? Looks like he first came here about five months ago, soon after we opened. And then more recently."

"How recently?"

"He was here four nights last week and most of Sunday."

"How'd he do?" Abel asked.

The manager shrugged.

Abel sighed. "One more box to check and I'm on my way home."

The manager picked up the phone and asked somebody named Chase to come to his office, then told Abel they kept charts for customers to track their progress. Soon Chase retrieved a flash drive with Crawford's information, deposited Abel at a laptop, and left him scrolling through row after row of bull's-eye targets. Each was labeled with a date and time; an X marked the spot where a bullet had hit the target. Five months ago, Brad's target accuracy was mediocre at best. Last week his accuracy improved steadily; by Sunday, he looked like an expert shot. Abel recalled the time he'd shot a man straight through the heart. He'd had years of professional practice plus the ultimate motivation—to save Max. *Lucky? I don't think so, scumbag.*

Back at the station, he looked through the eyewitness accounts that had come in through his outreach to social media. Several were clearly wackos looking for fame and glory. He made appointments to interview three people who sounded credible based on what he could glean online. Then he made a surprise visit to Crawford's office.

* * *

When Max arrived at his house the next evening, a Friday, he was ready to go meet her real-estate client.

Max shook her head. "She's not home."

"What, the Realtor's on a date with her killer boyfriend?"

"Don't joke. She's 'visiting her sick mom.' Total BS about her mom, but she did leave town."

"She's spooked?"

"Of course she's spooked! Her boyfriend-client faked a road-rage incident so he could eliminate the competition for a house he wanted."

"We detectives say *allegedly faked.*"

"I thought that was journalists."

"Doesn't matter. I've already broken the rules by discussing the case with you."

"You mean it doesn't count that I helped you with an earlier case?"

She said it matter-of-factly, but her help was an act of courage so astounding that she'd ended up abducted by the murderer/drug lord and then bound and gagged while he instructed a henchman to rape her.

"If there's a trial," she continued, "my client doesn't want to testify—unless you can guarantee Crawford will be convicted and put away."

"We'll see about that. I know who she is. Even an out-of-shape detective can put two and two together with a badge and one question."

"For what it's worth, you look better than you did."

"Do I?" he asked hopefully. He'd been too lovesick to eat much of anything since her casserole visit.

She stood up, and he watched her walk to the window. It was dusk—the magic hour—and the setting sun did not disappoint. He knew full well it was the humans who kept messing up.

She turned back to him. "So what *do* you actually know?"

"A lot, but not enough to make an arrest." He told her about calling on Crawford at his company, FS Hi-Tech Solutions.

"FS?"

"Fail Safe. The solutions they offer include security for a company's computer networks so they don't get hacked. Crawford's a hotshot at his company, and I figure he'd be smart enough to put a tracking device on Sanchez's car."

"I was told the closing date on the Preston Hollow house was sixty days out, so Brad would have had time to figure out Sanchez's routine. How does tracking work—with a phone app?"

"That's one way. He might've had one on his own phone. I don't have enough evidence for a warrant to take and examine it. Besides, he could've used a burner phone."

"So, a dead end?"

"Probably."

He told her about finding the shooting range where Crawford perfected his aim.

Max brightened. "That should be a nail in the case against him."

"If only. Cool as shaved ice, Crawford tells me he'd been invited to a 'shooting party' this weekend and was practicing so he wouldn't look like a fool."

"Who practices with a handgun to go hunting?"

"Not hunting. Shooting at targets set up on a big piece of land out in the country. The story checks out. I spoke to the guy hosting the party and drove out to see for myself."

She frowned. "And Brad didn't tell you this initially because it would look too suspicious? He perfects his shot and kills a man two days later."

"How'd you get so smart?"

"School of Hard Knocks. But you know that."

"One of the many fascinating things I know about you." He gave her a smoldering look, but she wouldn't bite.

"One piece of good news," he said. "College kid, twenty-one, driving home to Allen, saw what appears to be the start of the whole thing. The Porsche was in the middle lane doing the speed limit. A white Tesla—Crawford's car—comes up fast from behind and rams the back of the Porsche."

"And then?"

"Neither car broke down, so the kid figured the two drivers would stop and exchange insurance info. Went on his way."

"Sounds promising."

"Mmm. I'm talking to another eyewitness tomorrow. Max, I need you to fill in some blanks."

"Blanks?"

"How did Crawford know Sanchez was getting the house? That stuff's supposed to stay confidential until the property changes hands."

"I really need to go," she said.

"Look, Crawford's not just a murderer. He's some kind of psychopath, putting this amount of planning and cunning into killing a stranger over a house. Do you really want somebody like that free to do whatever the hell he pleases? Does the Realtor?"

She sighed and told him what he needed to know. That Brad had gone to his Realtor's office, instead of her apartment, to pick her up for their date. This was right after he didn't get the house. He asked if he could use her laptop to take care of something work-related. With his computer skills, he could have found the listing agent's correspondence or even the contract on the house. With Sanchez's name and address in hand, he would have had sixty days to figure out a plan.

Abel walked Max to the door. "Thank you," he said.

"FS Hi-Tech Solutions?"

"Max, don't even think about making another citizen's arrest."

"I'm not. I never carry a gun anymore."

"Wise move. Look, I probably acted like a jerk around you, but I get where you're at. I'm just glad we had this time together."

"Abel, don't you know you'll always be my hero?"

"*Always* seems a little over-the-top."

"And to think I once thought your blue eyes looked too good to be true."

She reached for him, and suddenly life was amazingly wonderful after all.

He swept her off her feet—just like in the movies!—and floated to the bedroom.

● ● ●

Abel lit another cigarette. It was Thursday, nine days since he got the call about the road-rage killing—and six days since he'd taken Max to bed. The clock said one a.m., but he wasn't on call so he poured himself a shot of whiskey and drank it down. It didn't sit right with all the cigarettes, maybe because he already had a cancerous tumor growing in the pit of his stomach, in solidarity with the malignant growth in his heart. He pictured

Max as she'd looked last night, glancing back at him with longing before she walked away, this time, she assured him, forever.

The case was dead too. The DA didn't want to prosecute. The eyewitness accounts of the road-rage incident contradicted one another. No evidence had turned up of anyone planting a tracking device on Sanchez's Porsche. (Crawford had been crouching by the Porsche when the police arrived. Abel figured that's when he removed it.) The Realtor-girlfriend had moved out of state to care for her ailing mother; besides, she had only wonderful things to say about her client. As for Crawford, he withdrew his offer on the house, saying it wasn't all that great for the price. He preferred California and had a better job waiting for him there. Abel had confronted him about all his lies—the in-your-face kind and the lies of omission—but the guy never cracked.

Abel threw the shot glass across the room. It didn't break, but it did puncture the drywall. His rage felt as big as a Texas tornado, but it had nowhere to go until he picked up the lamp and hurled it across the room and then started in on all the furniture.

He'd become a policeman for the right reasons: to help the helpless and stop the madness. But now he fully understood all the rage. The road of life was littered with it. Rage at not getting what you wanted when you knew your happiness depended on it.

Life was short and the happy part even shorter, and so much of the madness was beyond anyone's control. The universe was a marauding gorilla, and he felt like an ant underfoot.

PAM MCWILLIAMS has called Dallas home for many years. The story "Road Rage" is an offshoot of "Two-Legged Creatures," which appeared in volume one of this anthology series: two unrelated characters from the first story reconnect— and much has happened in the interim. Pam's other short stories include "Love is a Four Letter Word" and "The Fandango." She's a past president of Sisters in Crime North Dallas and co-hosts an after-school book club at an elementary school in South Dallas. Pam blogs about the Arts at "Shouts from a Third Act." www.shoutsfromathirdact.com

THE MYSTERIOUS DISAPPEARNCE OF JASON WHETSTONE

By Karen Harrington

In 2015, a talented mediator disappeared on his way to work. Months later, his remains were found inside the childhood home of one of his clients. Those responsible now sit in prison, one maintaining innocence. To this day, there are lingering questions. Reporters from *The Garlandian* look back on the chilling case.

This article is the second of an eight-part series about strange crimes in Garland, Texas.

● ● ●

Despite the calendar inching toward Valentine's Day, Christmas lights still outlined a few houses in Jason Whetstone's tree-lined Richardson neighborhood. With Whetstone's portfolio, he could have afforded an updated Tudor near his office in upscale University Park. But his associates said the humble, compact, detail-oriented man liked to be underestimated. And that he was the last person to be involved in any kind of crime.

This made his disappearance all the more baffling.

The day he vanished was like any other day for the fifty-five-year-old. He left his house in his usual go-to-work uniform: bespoke vest over button-down shirt with a tumbler of black coffee in hand. His calendar revealed that he had an early-morning appointment as the fundraising chair for a foster-based dog-rescue group. He slid into the leather seats of his Lexus sedan. The doorbell camera across the street from Whetstone's home recorded him backing out and driving away around five-thirty. He never made it to his destination.

In the weeks leading up to his disappearance, Whetstone's newest clients—two sisters—had become embroiled in a growing social-media spectacle. Whetstone was a senior partner at The Remedy Clinic, a cottage business aimed at helping Dallasites discreetly settle odd disputes before they entered the court system or drained their bank accounts—or both. Its founder, Dr. Erik Kellog, hired skilled mediators like Whetstone to act as part legal gymnast, part therapist.

"Our range of services and remedies are sometimes unusual, but then, so are the client issues," Kellog said. "Whetstone occasionally added a rescue animal to a prescribed remedy. He was that kind of guy. Very caring."

The Stratham sisters had the kind of knotty, petty issue Whetstone was skilled at untangling. The dispute centered on a family memory and who was telling the truth about it. While this kind of debate might be hashed out at a family Thanksgiving gathering, the Stratham sisters' feud was uniquely public. Both sisters were novelists. And each had written her version of the truth.

What the sisters did agree on was this: Twenty-five years earlier, when the girls were sixteen and fourteen, there was an argument with their mother about why her portion of spaghetti meat sauce was smaller than everyone else's. After a furious debate erupted at the dinner table, Mother Stratham grabbed her car keys and her youngest, Michael, and stormed out of the house. Years later, each writer cast herself as responsible for the consequential family event—and then wrote about it. It was

Whetstone's job to listen to both sides and determine if there was memory overlap or a whiff of plagiarism, as one sister claimed.

The older sister's editor pointed them to the clinic after reading about a Whetstone case that made national news. It involved two neighbors' annual autumn conflict over falling leaves (the wind blew a voluminous number of dead leaves from Client A's yard into Client B's yard).

"Everyone can relate to this kind of situation, this unjust chore of someone else's leaves literally falling at your feet. For these men, it was leaves. But it wasn't really about the falling leaves," Whetstone once told a reporter. "It never is."

Whetstone let the neighbors thrash out their dispute before issuing a remedy: hire the same landscaping company to collect the leaves from both properties on one assigned day. The collection of leaves, Whetstone said, removed the need for conflict. The remedy drew ire from some as too simplistic or too unjust. But his clients accepted it and moved on. They'd each garnered support on social-networking app Nextdoor from hundreds of neighbors dealing with similar petty domestic issues.

"Whetstone had been smart enough to recognize that sympathy for a problem was a dose of medicine in itself," remarked Kellog.

Like the falling-leaves dispute, the case about gatekeeping a memory promised to be about more than meat sauce for Laura Stratham and Mona Stratham (who used the pen name Mona Moore).

Laura Stratham had left home at age eighteen to marry her blue-eyed high school sweetheart, Dave Fogel. The pair had an on-again, off-again relationship, but friends recalled that Dave's easy smile and charm constantly wooed Laura back. Noted for her long thick dark locks, Laura cut her hair to a pixie when the duo married, selling her healthy strands for money. While Dave finished trade school and Laura worked odd jobs, the newlyweds lived a hand-to-mouth kind of existence. Laura filled stacks of black-and-white composition books, always ready to capture a piece of dialogue. In Laura's memoir, she claimed Dave had a snarky way of introducing her to friends:

"He'd say, 'Be careful what you say. Laura might include it in her little stories.' He put the words *little stories* in air quotes. He called my scribbles a hobby, but that made me want to work harder. I'd gotten married, in part, to just get out. I never knew which version of Mother I'd find at home."

Dave was also captured on the pages of her fiction, following their affair-fueled breakup and tenuous legal battle over their only child, a daughter. Inside those early pages, there's a scene where the Dave-like character, Earl, packs his things and prepares to leave his crying wife, Lola. On their mantel, there's a wooden heart, each of their names carved into one side. The names interlocked like two puzzle pieces. Lola broke it apart and threw half the heart at Earl.

"That really happened," Dave said. "She wanted me to take my piece, and I wanted her to keep it together. I was a jerk for having an affair, okay, but she did still love me. She did."

Laura adjusted to a new life as a single parent. "I was either working or writing in the library with my daughter. She read books and I wrote. The mac-and-cheese days."

Years later, Laura's mac-and-cheese days were behind her. She not only enjoyed bestseller status, she also became a hit on the writers-conference circuit. She found herself reciting entertaining vignettes about her childhood and early marriage.

"There was a market for her rags-to-riches journey," said her longtime editor, Soozi Finkels. "She was intrigued by the project and dove in, pen first."

The memoir, a rambling portrait of the Stratham family, gave praise to a dysfunctional childhood for toughening Laura. The opening pages showed her father, a high school science teacher, taking the family for a ride on a Sunday afternoon only to be left stranded hours later in a small town because he hadn't bothered to check the gas gauge. Worse, he didn't have any money so he asked the kids to panhandle on the side of the road while their mother napped in the car.

Laura wrote that it was the first time she learned that her family didn't always have her best interests at heart. "Part of writing the memoir was making sense of the past, which is why I included the meat-sauce story. When my mother got angry at me that night, it adversely impacted our entire family. I was just sixteen. Mother flew into a rage after surveying the entire dining table and decreeing that she'd been shorted meat sauce. She left with our ten-year-old brother, Michael, and lived in a motel for a month."

It didn't take long for news of Laura's memoir to reach her sister Mona. Inside Jason Whetstone's mediation-interview records, obtained exclusively by *The Garlandian,* Mona stated, "I've avoided reading Laura's work. Some people might like it, but it felt so crafted to me. Just not my thing. I guess there's a market for stories like that."

Whetstone replied, "Stories like what?"

"Her writing is to literature what fast food is to a gourmet meal. Digestible and forgettable."

"But you read it and that's how you formed this opinion?"

"I didn't need to read everything to know. And, besides, many of my friends and readers filled me in."

Years earlier, Mona had penned *Downward*, a novel that included a family argument at the dinner table. The fictional uproar led to the death of the matriarch, who fled the table in tears, grabbed her car keys, and soon after was involved in a fatal accident. Though Mona hadn't risen to the acclaim of her sister, her eagle-eyed readers noted the striking similarities in *Downward* and parts of Laura's memoir.

"The scene where the mama gets angry over meat sauce, blames the daughter, and leaves the family? It's the same in each book," one reviewer wrote.

Mona was puzzled. Why would Laura falsely write that she was the one who'd angered their mother that night? And since *Downward* was published five years before Laura's memoir, was this more than stealing a memory—was this also plagiarism?

"It was me who angered our mother and set her off," Mona said.

Whetstone questioned her. "And you want to own the fact that you alone angered your mother? Slighted her dinner plate?"

"I own it because it's the truth," Mona answered. "You can't claim someone else's childhood trauma as your own. And that's what Laura has done. Though my fictional mother died, it was like the death of our family after that night."

Both sisters' works described a home in which the matriarch was unpredictable and eccentric. She refused to buy living room furniture. She painted all the time. The Stratham family of Laura's memoir and the characters in Mona's novel sit in white-and-green lawn chairs facing a huge wooden television set. There was also a modern black-and-white mural in various stages of completion. Laura wrote, "Our mother was always painting on small canvases, but the mural that dominated the dining room wall was a never-ending geometric work in progress."

Like Laura, Mona dreamed of a way out and up. A red-headed beauty with hazel eyes, Mona was famished for attention and validation, friends said. Where Laura chased after a youthful romance to escape a dysfunctional home, Mona saw herself in Paris cafés, writing and observing. She got as far as Iowa, earning a prized spot at the Iowa Writers' Workshop. Associates remember her as kind, teacherly, ever ready for a public reading or critique session. She loved hosting late-night happy hours. Members of the writing community called her "Queen" because of the way she loved to hold court.

"There was a book that outlined the inspirations of something like fifty famous writers," a former classmate recalled. "She knew all of those origin stories and would orate them again and again. It was over-the-top, but she'd look into your face and compare your writing to a legend, pulling out a pearl of a sentence and praising its beauty. How could you not like that kind of adulation? It was a little like taking a drug while knowing it's bad for you."

After the term at the Iowa workshop ended, Mona's options were thin. She took a job in Southeast Oklahoma as an insurance adjuster. She held nighttime critique groups, helping others workshop their stories while getting feedback on her own. When *Downward* was published, she sent copies to all of her family members.

"They had the book, and they didn't respond," Mona wrote on her blog. "Maybe it was because I'd pulled a lot from my life, our life, and put it on the page. It was healing for me. If they wanted to keep their distance, fine."

But it wasn't really fine. When Laura sold her debut in a splashy two-book deal two years later, Mona reached out with congratulations and an offer to do book events together. (By then, Mona had self-published a new book of linked short stories about Oklahoma tornado survivors.) Laura took a while to reply to Mona's offer. "I think my publicist is working all that out. I hope you'll come to an event! Would be great to see you," Laura wrote in a short text to Mona.

Mona responded, "Why don't you want to see me? Why don't you want to get together? All my friends have solid relationships with their sisters. I don't understand. What have I done, Laura?"

Her questions went unanswered.

Laura's debut released to praise, her sophomore follow-up garnered even more fans, and then came her popular memoir. Soon after the memoir hit the shelves, Mona launched a series of Facebook posts devoted to the stolen meat-sauce story. Her fans took her side and began pummeling review sites with scathing one-star reviews of Laura's books.

In one of Mona's Facebook posts, she wrote:

"My dear friends know that there was a period in my life that devastated me. I've written about it privately most of my life. And to find out that it had been written about so publicly and without my knowledge in the pages of Laura Stratham's book. Is there any civility anymore? I mean, what would you do if someone took your precious memories and monetized them for personal gain? We've sought a professional referee to help us with this issue, but I fear the truth will never see the light unless all parties are accountable."

Laura seemed to have taken the bait of her sister's social-media provocation. A short while later, she stated in an interview, "It's ridiculous to say I plagiarized anything from Mona. Some of our experiences overlap. She doesn't get to gatekeep our childhood memories."

This is when Laura's editor, who'd read about the falling-leaves saga, persuaded her to take the issue to Whetstone at The Remedy Clinic.

"I hoped it might quickly settle things," Finkels said. "I'd read his book too, and it seemed like its wisdom applied."

Whetstone had penned a pithy, pocket-size book on his tips for settling disagreements with chapters including:

What is Your End Goal?

What does Winning Mean to You?

Prioritize Peace over Being Right

It was recommended reading for his clients.

"The Strathams couldn't be bothered to read the book," said Dean Ray Vanderbilt, The Remedy Clinic's attorney. "Jason was fond of saying that people don't want an apology or money. They want a time machine. And once they realize that's not possible, Jason often led them to a peaceful resolution. But it took time to get there."

A month before Whetstone's disappearance, the Stratham sisters' dispute stalled. Vanderbilt hinted that Whetstone had presented three options to the embattled sisters, one capitalizing on the increased notoriety and book sales both authors had enjoyed since the case went public.

"One of the sisters was incredulous that this might be seen as a remedy," Vanderbilt said.

Mona wrote in a post that nothing short of a full public admission of memory stealing was acceptable. Her followers on Twitter started a *#tellthetruthlaura* hashtag campaign. Laura confided in friends that she was annoyed by her sister's online antics.

Mona fired off a rapid succession of emails and texts, accusing Laura of purposely dragging out the mediation for dramatic effect. Most of them went unanswered by Laura. Interview records captured Mona's complaints to Whetstone about being ignored. "The nice thing to do would have been to let me sit on one of those author panels and discuss it with the public. Let the sunshine disinfect. Others could learn from our unique dynamic."

"Is that what you would like from this experience? To teach others?" Whetstone asked.

"It's lemonade from lemons now," Mona replied. "That's what Ike says, anyway."

At this point, the eldest Stratham sibling was drawn into the fray.

Ike Stratham is a tall good-natured man. A former Marine, he's now a physician assistant who often works with Doctors Without Borders. He had also been in charge of his father's estate. (Mother Stratham, who'd moved to nearby Plano following the divorce, preceded her former husband in death.) When his father died in 2005, Ike, fresh off a divorce, moved into the childhood home in Garland, dubbed The Submarine because of its bright-yellow brick and squat ranch-style architecture. Ike paid each of his siblings a share of its worth and sent them one of the old folding green-and-white lawn chairs.

Weeks after Mona and Laura engaged Whetstone's services, Mona visited Ike at The Submarine.

"Mona read both passages from both books out loud," Ike remembered. "Yes, they were very similar, I had to admit. But I'm no reader, and so I felt, one is non-fiction, one is fiction, what does it matter? Then Dave showed up, looking for a beer, and Mona asked him the same question."

Fogel, hit by financial downturn, had moved back to his parents' Garland house, a block from The Submarine, and was still friendly with most of the Strathams.

"He was on her side," Ike said. "You should have seen Mona. She was thrilled."

Soon after, Mona moved her diary of the meat-sauce issue to an exclusive blog, called *My Beef*. She led it off with a summation of the case and a quasi-interview with Dave about his experiences with Laura. It rehashed his resentment about being cast as disloyal, dimwitted fictional Earl, giving readers of the *#tellthetruthlaura* hashtag the chance to see that "Laura wasn't afraid to use or trash her family to get ahead."

"Mona got Dave to side with her because they were both upset with Laura," Ike said. "But the book stuff was ridiculous, and I believed this Whetstone guy could referee it quickly. But when he didn't, I invited them to The Sub to talk."

Ultimately, the sisters' dispute could not be solved at the oak dining table inside The Submarine, where the contested event occurred so long ago. "And it all blew up, anyway, because we found out that Laura was recording our conversation."

This fact found its way onto Mona's blog.

Looking back, Vanderbilt remembered how Mona pleaded with him for permission to post the full transcript of her private sessions with Whetstone. When he refused, she wrote her own version.

"It was difficult to understand why Mona believed this cast her in a positive light," said Vanderbilt. "Unless we consider that it kept the drama going and provided additional fodder for her readership."

Blog Entry, March 28

Dear Readers, I'm sharing insights into my mediation with my sister at The Remedy Clinic. See for yourself what it's like to be interviewed by Jason Whetstone. We're still praying he's found safe and we can resume our discussions.

Mona (Stratham) Moore, Interview 1

Mona: I'm hoping this will be a swift mediation, because I think the press has wind of it or soon will. I desperately want to show a united front should we have to talk to a reporter, you know? I only want justice.

Whetstone: Justice?

Mona: The fact is, Laura's been usurping from our family for some time. I'm utterly crushed.

Whetstone: How do you mean?

Mona: She lifts from everyone's life.

Whetstone: Arguably, the work of all writers.

Mona: This is much different.

Whetstone: How so?

Mona: My friends read her stuff, and they have questions for ME. Can you imagine? Anyone related to a writer, take heed. Have you spoken to Dave, her ex?

Whetstone: No.

Mona: Well, you should. But the fact is that she misused MY story. My parents' vicious fight started over the lack of meat sauce, specifically on my mother's plate. She believed I'd purposely cheated her. I hadn't noticed, that I remember. Why would I short her on meat sauce? My own beloved mother. She had a tremendous outburst. She often had flare-ups with me. We had the worst relationship, but I keep that private, except from my closest friends. That night, my dad jumped in to quell the argument. Suddenly forks were flying. Before I knew it, she moved out with Michael. All because of what I did. My action helped end our happy family. And Michael? His life was irretrievably broken by it. Destroyed. I think back and wonder, did I do that on purpose? But I wouldn't do that. Perhaps the best way to illustrate this is by reading the scene from my book.

Whetstone: There's no need. I already reviewed both books.

Mona: But I really feel…

Whetstone: No, that won't be necessary.

Mona: I see.

Whetstone: I'm curious about one thing, Mona. You have four siblings. Michael, Ike, Laura, and Claire. No mention of Claire in this memory?

Mona: Well, I don't know. I don't know why that is. But I need you to understand what I wrote.

Whetstone: Let's shift gears a bit. Laura wrote a scene where the kids had to panhandle for gas money. Do you recall that day?

Mona: Laura sat on the curb and let Ike do most of the work.

Whetstone: But that vignette, that memory, she remembered and recorded it correctly.

Mona: I guess.

Whetstone: You see where I'm going here?

Mona: Just because she got some things right doesn't validate her entire account.

With the help of Vanderbilt, *The Garlandian* accessed the actual mediation transcript from this interview. They are identical, suggesting that Mona had secretly recorded her session. She would never confirm or deny this action.

Throughout the years, Laura and Mona had little contact with their other sister, Claire. Claire moved a lot, and her whereabouts were difficult to track. Now a chef for a posh Las

Vegas eatery, Claire had responded to an email from Whetstone, saying, "I'm the middle child. That's all you need to know about why they haven't talked much about me. My brothers either. As much as it might be fun to watch them continue paying you hefty fees, which I pray they are, this will all be solved if you ask them about Brenda."

Here, Whetstone might have ended the conflict between the two sisters by inviting them to consider what happened with the mysterious Brenda. But why didn't he?

Vanderbilt speculated that Whetstone was determined to let Mona and Laura reach an epiphany. "He loved seeing people round that corner independently, though I can't say if that was his plan," Vanderbilt offered. "I encouraged him to verify Brenda's existence and settle the case. It's fair to say that at this point in the mediation, Jason and I didn't know about Mona's numerous posts or the anti-Laura Twitter hashtag. He would have called foul on that, I'm certain."

As it turned out, Brenda was real.

She was a childhood neighbor. If the Strathams were scraping by, Brenda's family was poorer still. Her father sold her cat for a carton of cigarettes. She was often seen drinking water from the outdoor hose. Whatever eccentricities Mother Stratham exhibited, she made it known that Brenda could come in and out of The Submarine whenever she pleased. What no one but Claire had observed was Brenda sneaking in, helping herself to a few bites from one of the bowls on the day of the infamous meat-sauce argument, then slinking out just as quickly. The story of Brenda's easy access to the kitchen was corroborated by Ike Stratham.

"Oh, yes, Brenda," Ike told Whetstone in a phone call the week before he disappeared. "She was a slip of a girl."

Whetstone probed a little further, asking Ike if he thought the revelation of Brenda's visit would help end his sisters' quarrel over the meat-sauce tale.

"Honestly? No, I think they are going to push this to the bitter end."

Indeed, Ike was prescient.

The sisters would ramp up their efforts to continue the battle on their respective social-media sites.

When news that Mona had published an excerpt of one of her Whetstone sessions reached Laura, she shot back with a post on her website.

Dear Readers,

I'm unhappily drawn into this public spectacle with my sister. If you want to learn my version of events as related to Mona and this particular incident, you can find those details in my memoir within the chapter titled "Mother Takes Michael."

Recently *The Garlandian* wrote to younger brother Michael at his address at a Texas correctional facility to get his perspective on the family drama. His only response to the meat-sauce night was this:

"My parents fought at dinner all the time. My mother required an audience. My sisters are nuts. My mother packed up and left The Submarine and took me with her. That this was all about meat sauce is crazy. People do shit and break up. I think they have lost the plot. Even if I was free, I wouldn't set foot at a Thanksgiving table with those two. One day I'd had too much to drink and was a jerk at my father's birthday party. I left on foot. Laura chased me down an alley, and I told her, I said, 'All you want is material for your novel.' That's probably true, but she was also trying to give me a ride home. You never know with writers. They are always stealing."

Michael Stratham is serving a two-year sentence for theft.

In one of Whetstone's last notes in the Stratham file, he mused in the margins. "Interesting that Mother Stratham easily shared food with Brenda but made a family fight out of it as well. Proof of falling-leaves theory?"

Thinking back on the events, Vanderbilt remembered having growing concern about The Remedy Clinic's reputation getting tarnished by the drawn-out drama. Hoping to put the case to rest and focus on Whetstone's disappearance, he arranged and recorded a Skype call with the sisters to discuss Brenda.

Transcript of final minutes of Skype call between Mona and Laura.

Laura: Brenda. Do you remember her? I guess that's that.

Mona: What do you mean?

Laura: It means that Brenda probably ate some of the meat sauce.

Mona: I doubt it very much.

Laura: Well, you got what you wanted. We went for a remedy and now it's done. We know what must have really happened.

Mona: I don't accept that. You stole my story. Tell the truth, Laura!

Laura: Oh, yes, your fancy little hashtag.

Mona: I can't help what my fans do.

Laura: Fans?

Vanderbilt: Authorities will be reaching out if they have more questions about Jason.

Skype call ends.

From this point, Mona's serialized journey from starving artist to justice seeker took on a new component. She promised to tell more of the family secrets and concluded each post with an admonition to her readers to read both of the sister-writers' works and provided links to stores from which signed copies of her novel, *Downward*, could be ordered. Each post teased readers that the conclusion of the mediation would be forthcoming "as soon as our mediator, Jason Whetstone, is found safe and resumes his work." She began monetizing her blog, adding a link to a Patreon account to fund her artistic works. She never updated her readers with the revelation about Brenda.

Laura quietly went back to work on a new novel. She attended a writers' conference where she dodged questions about her sister's serialized story. "I'm much more interested in the serious concern of where our adviser and friend, Jason Whetstone, is and if he is safe."

As April rains descended upon North Texas, the case broke open.

Laura received a panicked call from her daughter. "Mom, Mom, check the news. Something to do with that missing guy. He's dead."

Laura did a quick search on her phone and pulled up a disturbing article.

Missing Richardson man found dead

Noted mediator and Richardson resident Jason Whetstone, who went missing earlier this year, was found dead Monday afternoon, said a spokesman from the Garland Police Department.

Around 1 p.m., GPD officers were dispatched to a home in the 4500 block of Clairmont Drive after a body was found. The body was later identified as Whetstone, officials said. His cause of death is unknown.

"The homeowner, Ike Stratham, returned from an extended trip and discovered the grisly scene. He did not immediately know the identity of the victim," police said.

Stratham told police he'd hired a neighbor, David Fogel, 41, as a house sitter.

A subsequent search of Fogel's house and garage led to the recovery of Whetstone's car.

"Fogel admitted he abducted Whetstone at gunpoint three months prior and drove him to Stratham's house," police said.

Fogel was arrested on kidnapping charges, with other charges pending. An autopsy will be conducted, and the death remains under investigation.

After three months, the long search for Whetstone was over. Laura texted Ike, "What's going on?"

She got no answer. She texted Dave and Mona. All her texts and calls went unanswered.

Mona was silent and for good reason. She'd known the location of Jason Whetstone from day one. And she'd been having an affair with his kidnapper, Dave Fogel.

A man torn between two novelists, Fogel quickly became an open book.

Fogel told police that when the affair started, he was between jobs and had loads of time on his hands. He drove up to Durant, Oklahoma, to visit Mona. What began as a supportive friendship quickly spiraled into a passionate tryst. Dave spent days with Mona, doing odd jobs around her house, visiting the local casino in the evenings. He was about to head to Hochatown, Oklahoma, to do repair work on cabins when he half joked to Mona that for the right price, he'd take Whetstone along with him and pressure him to side in her favor, vindicating her original claim of ownership to the childhood drama and "to get back at Laura." Mona "liked the idea instantly," Fogel said. He canceled plans to head to Hochatown, because Mona suggested they hide Whetstone at The Submarine.

"Ike was out of town for a volunteer gig in Honduras," Fogel told police. "He'd asked me to keep an eye on the house. All I had to do was get Whetstone there."

Days after Fogel returned to Garland, he was busy casing Whetstone's neighborhood, aiming to find an ideal spot to overtake the mediator at gunpoint. His planning worked. That fateful February morning, Fogel took an Uber to Whetstone's neighborhood. At a stop sign, Fogel demanded entry to Whetstone's car. Then he instructed Whetstone to power off his phone and drive to Garland.

They parked inside The Submarine's garage. Fogel then locked and barricaded Whetstone inside a bedroom, but not before giving him a sedative.

Later, he received a text from Mona.

Mona: Do you have him?

Dave: Yes.

Mona: Laura's gonna freak out, and I'm here for it.

Dave: What next?

Mona: I'll take care of it.

Fogel was unsure how to interpret that, only that he thought Mona would be the next person to visit The Submarine.

"I'd done my part. I moved his car to my house. Mona was going to, you know, interview him or something. After another week had passed, she wouldn't tell me how she'd taken care of Whetstone, only that I shouldn't worry about him," Fogel said.

For better or worse, Fogel's internet search history revealed that he was still thinking of it. On day eight, he'd searched: *how long can someone survive without food.*

It would be the early return of Ike Stratham that unveiled the truth about Whetstone.

"I came home to a horror. A horrible smell came from the back room. A sense I wasn't alone." He entered the hallway, found a locked door, and kicked it in. Ike rang the police, then Fogel. Fogel, he said, issued several expletives and broke down on the phone, saying he needed to talk to Mona. Mona, he cried out to Ike, knew all about it.

Fogel walked from his own house to The Submarine. He was arrested on the porch, where he had once come to pick up Laura for dates.

"I didn't think this would happen," he said to officers. "I didn't think anyone would get hurt. Mona said she'd take care of it."

While investigators collected evidence at The Submarine, Ike sent Mona more than thirty texts filled with questions and accusations.

As her phone blew up, Mona spent three hours typing up a final chapter for her blog and scheduled it to post automatically at a future date. Then she texted Ike that she was on her way and was aghast at what Dave had done.

Ike recalls that she wrote in all caps, "I'M COMPLETELY SHOCKED!"

Next, she drove to the house where Ike, Laura, local police, and Vanderbilt had gathered.

"I wanted to see her face," Vanderbilt said. "To look her in the eye for Jason. She was stone cold."

A long night unraveled for the Stratham family. Ike, whose bag was still packed from his trip, hunkered down across town with Laura.

"We mourn the loss of this talented man and will pray he didn't suffer and his killers will be brought to justice," Kellog said to a TV news reporter.

The investigation moved swiftly, though Mona remained silent.

"She wouldn't talk to anyone but her attorney," Ike said. "She stared at the floor when I asked her if she was sorry that she'd ruined Dave's life and caused Whetstone's death. And, not inconsequentially, the fact that my house was ruined."

Ike had already begun to think of having The Submarine razed.

"All Mona would say was that she couldn't help who fell in love with her and what they'd do for love," Ike said.

According to the medical examiner, Whetstone had been dead for months when Ike found him. Authorities wouldn't immediately comment on the contents of the deadly drug cocktail. However, court records would later reveal that Fogel administered a fatal dose of his parents' prescription medications.

Whetstone was quietly laid to rest, surrounded by friends from his dog-rescue group and several of his former clients, including the men from the falling-leaves case.

"He didn't deserve this," one of the men told *The Garlandian*. "What's wrong with people?"

While Fogel and Mona awaited their days in court, one final twist in the meat-sauce story surfaced.

Exactly a month after Mona's arrest, her *My Beef* blog spit out a new entry.

Dear Readers, by now, you may know about recent events and accusations in the case of Jason Whetstone's disappearance and David Fogel's involvement. Follow the steps below to read the full, untold account.

Readers were directed to a paywall, behind which they could read the latest entry in her ongoing blog series. One commenter said the long-form entry read "like an unintentionally comic romance." It expanded on her family and the tortured relationship with Fogel, on whom she laid full blame for Jason Whetstone's tragic death.

Readers swarmed the page, paying to read one of the last chapters of the Stratham family drama.

Mona was convicted of criminal conspiracy and felony murder. Fogel was convicted of felony kidnapping and felony murder. Mona's attorneys are working on an appeal.

The Garlandian questioned everyone in the case about why a writer would go to these unlawful lengths.

Vanderbilt puzzled it out. "I think Mona got what she wanted. Fame and a lot of sympathy. But it's her failure to accept any responsibility or show remorse that's troubling. There's no remedy for a person like that. Jason was right, you know. He would have said it was never really about the meat sauce."

KAREN HARRINGTON is a freelance writer and author from Texas. Her short work has appeared in *Shotgun Honey*, *Mystery Tribune*, and *Ellery Queen's Mystery Magazine*, where she won the 2021 Ellery Queen Mystery Magazine Readers Choice Award for "Boo Radley College Prep." Karen is the author of four novels, including *Sure Signs of Crazy*, a Kirkus Best Book of the Year, and *Mayday*, a Lone Star Reading List pick. "The Strange Disappearance of Jason Whetstone" is one of a series of stories featuring the fictional Remedy Clinic. Another entry, "Would You Like A Remedy?," appears in the March/April 2023 issue of *Alfred Hitchcock's Mystery Magazine*. Find her at www.karenharringtonbooks.com

ABOUT THE EDITOR AND JUDGES

J SUZANNE FRANK has published ten novels and several short stories. She taught in and managed a creative-writing program for adults for twenty years. Her books are: in time travel: *Reflections in the Nile, Shadows on the Aegean, Sunrise on the Mediterranean,* and *Twilight in Babylon*; in mystery: *Going Out In Style, Designed to Die,* and *Fashion Victim*; in fantasy: *When Fire Loves Water: Part I The Siren* and *When Fire Loves Water: Part II The Kiss Between Breaths*; in women's fiction, *Laws of Migration*. Suzanne writes in Dallas and teaches (occasional) workshops in Italy. Jsuzannefrank.com

BARB GOFFMAN is a short story writer and freelance crime-fiction editor. She's won the Agatha Award (twice), as well as the Macavity Award, Silver Falchion Award, and Readers Award given by *Ellery Queen's Mystery Magazine*. She's been nominated for major crime-writing awards thirty-seven times, including seventeen Agatha nominations (a category record), and multiple nominations for the Anthony, Macavity, and Derringer awards. Novels and stories she's edited have won the Agatha, Derringer, and EQMM Readers Award and have been nominated for the Agatha, Anthony, Derringer, Macavity, and Shamus awards. In 2020, *Crime Travel*, a time-travel mystery anthology Barb edited, was nominated for the Anthony. She blogs at SleuthSayers.org. Learn more at barbgoffman.com.

CAROLYN KIRK is a voracious reader and writes reviews for several publications. She is a former flight attendant, has a BS degree in Criminology & Corrections, and spent some time as a court-appointed special advocate. She divides her time between Texas and Maine, where she spends the summer months. When she's not reading, she's probably kayaking, hiking, or redecorating.

VALERIE WIGGLESWORTH spent more than thirty years working as a newspaper reporter and editor and produced some of her most memorable news stories while covering courts and crime in Texas. She continues to work as an editor in a variety of formats. Valerie is a big fan of mysteries, thrillers, and crime novels and often spends her free time settled in with a good book.